No Tea Party

Longarm let out a shout of warning and began to run toward the men, but he was too late. The messenger was knocked sprawling and then repeatedly stabbed by a trio of assassins. Longarm drew his gun and shouted. The three men each buried their knives into the fallen man one last time and then turned to attack Longarm.

Longarm's first shot struck the leader square in the chest and stopped him in his tracks, but with unbelievable determination and perhaps some kind of chemical help, the man recovered and staggered forward, raising his knife and screaming even louder. Longarm fired at the other two attackers and hit them both. Like the first, they slowed yet did not stop coming with their bloody knives held out in front of them and screams still on their foaming lips . . .

TABOR EVANS

LONGARM

AND THE DEADLY LOVER

JOVE BOOKS, NEW YORK

THE BERKLEY PUBLISHING GROUP
Published by the Penguin Group
Penguin Group (USA) Inc.
375 Hudson Street, New York, New York 10014, USA
Penguin Group (Canada), 90 Eglinton Avenue East, Suite 700, Toronto, Ontario M4P 2Y3, Canada
(a division of Pearson Penguin Canada Inc.)
Penguin Books Ltd., 80 Strand, London WC2R 0RL, England
Penguin Group Ireland, 25 St. Stephen's Green, Dublin 2, Ireland (a division of Penguin Books Ltd.)
Penguin Group (Australia), 250 Camberwell Road, Camberwell, Victoria 3124, Australia
(a division of Pearson Australia Group Pty. Ltd.)
Penguin Books India Pvt. Ltd., 11 Community Centre, Panchsheel Park, New Delhi—110 017, India
Penguin Group (NZ), Cnr. Airborne and Rosedale Roads, Albany, Auckland 1310, New Zealand
(a division of Pearson New Zealand Ltd.)
Penguin Books (South Africa) (Pty.) Ltd., 24 Sturdee Avenue, Rosebank, Johannesburg 2196,
South Africa

Penguin Books Ltd., Registered Offices: 80 Strand, London WC2R 0RL, England

This is a work of fiction. Names, characters, places, and incidents either are the product of the author's imagination or are used fictitiously, and any resemblance to actual persons, living or dead, business establishments, events, or locales is entirely coincidental.

LONGARM AND THE DEADLY LOVER

A Jove Book / published by arrangement with the author

PRINTING HISTORY
Jove edition / September 2006

Copyright © 2006 by The Berkley Publishing Group.

ISBN: 0-515-14201-8

JOVE®
Jove Books are published by The Berkley Publishing Group,
a division of Penguin Group (USA) Inc.,
375 Hudson Street, New York, New York 10014.
JOVE is a registered trademark of Penguin Group (USA) Inc.
The "J" design is a trademark belonging to Penguin Group (USA) Inc.

PRINTED IN THE UNITED STATES OF AMERICA

10 9 8 7 6 5 4 3 2 1

Chapter 1

Denver was gripped by an unusual cold spell through April, and everyone was talking about the light snow that had recently fallen across the city and how the edges of Cherry Creek were still rimmed with ice.

"It's a sign that the end of the world is coming," the Reverend Joshua Toliver was quoted in the newspaper. He had gone on to say, "The Bible tells us that the end will come soon with damnation and fire, but I believe that the end will come instead with ice and a cold so deep that the earth will be frozen in its sinful state for eternity. Mark my words, our time is near!"

But Deputy U.S. Marshal Custis Long didn't buy any of that as he trudged past the Denver Mint toward his federal office building. As far as he was concerned, a late winter was just what Colorado needed after being locked in a drought for three years straight.

"Marshal Long," a street urchin who sold newspapers said, thin face pinched with cold and worry. "Do you think that the Reverend Toliver is right about the world ending with cold and ice?"

Longarm shook his head even as he bought the morn-

1

ing's newspaper and saw the headlines predicting doom for the world. "No, Andrew, I don't think that the world is about to turn into a block of ice."

"But the Reverend is said to be a wise and learned man," Andrew argued. "And nobody . . . not even the old people . . . can remember winter lasting this long and hard."

"There is no explaining the weather," Longarm told the boy. "But one thing I do know is that it is always changing. The minute we think we can figure out what it will do next, it plays tricks on us."

"I dunno," Andrew said, taking the coin that Longarm handed him in exchange for the newspaper. "It just seems to me like I've been cold all my life. I sure would like to see a warm, sunny day. It would cheer me up considerably."

Longarm gave the boy another coin and laid his hand on Andrew's shoulder. "I tell you what," he said, bending because he was a tall man. "I predict that the sun will shine next week and the dark clouds will all go away. And then, in about two weeks, it'll be so warm that everyone will be complaining about the heat."

Andrew turned his dirty face upward and grinned. "I hope you're right, but the Reverend is—"

"A good man who likes to cause a stir and fill the pews in his church so he can get more money," Longarm interrupted. "Now you just wait and see which one of us is right."

"Yes, sir!" Andrew looked hopeful. "I just don't want to be cold anymore. It's been a long, hard winter."

"It has," Longarm agreed. "But the winter is about over . . . that much I promise."

Longarm continued along Colfax Avenue careful not to slip on the icy sidewalk. He was glad that he was able to lift Andrew's hopes and assure the lad that the world wasn't about to end with everyone and everything freezing solid. And he wished that preachers like Toliver wouldn't keep making such predictions of doom. But then again, they needed followers and nothing brought in sinners and the faint of heart quicker than the prophecy that the world was about to end.

"Marshal Vail would like to see you," the secretary told Longarm when he arrived at his office. "Custis, it seems to be a matter of some urgency."

"Thank you," Longarm told the woman. "And did you have a nice weekend?"

"No. It was too cold and I'm scared to death that Reverend Toliver's prediction is about to come true."

"Oh, bosh! Listen, Emily, the sun will shine again and soon enough we'll all be griping about the heat."

"I'd like to believe that," Emily said. "I really would. But the Reverend might be onto something."

Longarm knew that Mrs. Emily Harris was one who preferred to worry about anything and everything. Some people just couldn't stop fretting, and they'd be that way until their last breath.

"Mornin' Billy," Longarm said, walking into his boss's office. "I understand that you wanted to see me right away."

"You're late as usual," Billy said, pulling out his pocket watch. "Nine o'clock and the morning is half over already."

Marshal Billy Vail was always grumpy first thing in the morning, which is why Longarm tried to ignore the man. "What crisis are we facing today?"

"Have a seat," Billy ordered.

"Custis," Billy said, leaning back in his office chair. "Did you read today's paper?"

"If you're going to tell me about the Reverend Toliver predicting that we'll all freeze to death and the world will end, I don't need to hear it."

3

"No," Billy said, looking peeved, "what I was referring to was the fact that none other than our Denver chief of police, Robert Muldoon, was beaten so savagely that he is not expected to survive. Not only that, but his wife was also beaten and . . . and it appears that she was *raped*."

Longarm blinked with surprise and outrage. "Where!"

"At their home."

"And their children?"

"Both of the children were asleep in their upstairs bedrooms and were left undisturbed, thank God."

Longarm's fists clenched until the knuckles turned white. "When were Bob and his wife . . ."

"They were both found this morning by the family maid. Mr. Muldoon was unconscious and his wife had been so brutalized that she is still unable to speak. The report I received said that she is deep in shock."

"The city police will be all over that house and the neighborhood looking for whoever did this."

"I know that," Billy said. "You and the Muldoons were well acquainted, were you not?"

"Yes," Longarm said, his mood turning dark with anger. "I was honored by their friendship and value it highly."

"That's what I thought," Billy said. "Both of them are in the hospital and I don't know if they'll survive. I've only just received a report, and apparently Mrs. Muldoon is beyond hysteria. Friends are coming to stay at their bedsides and everyone is praying that they will recover. But at this time, things do not look promising."

Longarm was so upset he could not sit, so he jumped up and began to pace back and forth in front of Billy's desk as his boss kept talking.

"So far, there are no suspects. No one was seen entering the Muldoon residence nor were they seen leaving. There is no sign of theft."

Longarm stopped pacing. "Nothing taken?"

"No," Billy said. "Not that anyone can determine so far."

"Then this was about *revenge*."

Billy shrugged his round shoulders. "That is what seems most likely, but it is obviously far too soon to make that judgment."

"What else could it be?"

"I don't know," Billy conceded, "but I'm sure that we can count on a full investigation into this horrible crime. The city police will leave no stone unturned in their quest to find the person or persons responsible for these heinous acts."

"I hope that . . ." Longarm decided not to finish.

"Hope what?" Billy asked.

"That Emily Muldoon was not violated in the way that you suggest."

"Me, too," Billy said, choosing not to meet Longarm's penetrating gaze. "However, she was found naked and battered on the parlor rug."

"Damn!"

"Precisely," Billy said. "Custis, I know this *isn't* a federal matter, but since you were close to the family, I would like you to go over there and offer any assistance to the family or to the investigation that we can provide. And I mean *any* assistance."

"I'm on my way," Longarm said.

"But don't interfere," Billy cautioned. "This despicable outrage was against the city's police chief and the city police will be tireless and relentless in their pursuit of justice."

"I know that."

"Then," Billy said, "you know well enough to leave them to their own justice."

"Yes," Longarm said, "unless they hit a dead end and can't solve the crime. In that case I assume that—"

"We'll cross that bridge if we have to," Billy said. "But I'll tell you this. Whoever is responsible had better be smart enough to leave town because the Denver police will not rest until they've turned over every stone."

"Yeah," Longarm agreed. "There are some good investigators in the Denver Police Department. I wouldn't be surprised if they are already making arrests."

"Let's hope so. And pray that Chief Muldoon and his lovely wife make a complete and rapid recovery."

"Amen to that," Longarm said as he stomped out the door.

Chapter 2

Longarm was in a dark and dangerous mood when he arrived at Denver's largest hospital and was then refused entry to see Bob and Emily Muldoon.

"They're upstairs fighting for their lives right now," a tall police lieutenant explained after detaching himself from a crowd of other concerned officers. "The doctors say that no one can see the chief or his wife."

"What are their chances?" Longarm asked.

The lieutenant's face was grave. "I'm afraid not good. The chief is barely hanging onto life by a thread. Mrs. Muldoon is better, but not out of the woods by any means. The doctors say that she's in deep shock along with having been badly abused."

"Any idea yet of who did this?"

"Not a clue," the lieutenant spat in anger. "But we'll find the man or men who did this to our boss. Right now, we're canvassing their neighborhood asking anyone and everyone if they saw any suspicious characters around the Muldoon house."

Longarm removed his brown hat with its flat brim and

angrily twisted it in his powerful hands. "Lieutenant," he asked, "exactly when do you think the break-in happened?"

The lieutenant shrugged. "Sometime last evening and probably after midnight. The children were sleeping in another room. They didn't see or hear anything. Maybe that's a blessing in one respect."

Longarm nodded. "Yes, I understand. But if it happened at night, I doubt that you'll find any witnesses."

"We'll see."

"What about enemies?" Longarm asked.

"The chief had a bunch of 'em as you'd expect," the lieutenant said. "He was relentless in ordering our department to hunt down criminals. I expect that we've hanged at least twenty men since he took office. The figure could be higher. He worked his way up from the streets here, so he made a lot of arrests long before he was promoted up through the ranks."

Longarm's gray eyes narrowed. "And I'm sure that you're checking out the friends and families involved?"

"We're already getting started. We'll have a dozen police officers canvassing the city tracking down any surviving relatives and friends of people that the chief considered undesirables or enemies."

The lieutenant shook his head. "But without witnesses or any evidence, we don't have a lot of hope of getting whoever done this unless we happen to get real lucky."

"Make your own luck," Longarm said.

"Sure." The lieutenant studied the other anxious policemen all standing around the hospital waiting room hoping for good news about the Muldoons. Then he turned back to Longarm. "I understand that you were good friends with the family."

"That's right."

The lieutenant studied Longarm closely. "You aren't

thinking of getting involved in this case, are you, Marshal Long?"

"Only if you can't solve it," Longarm said, looking straight into the man's eyes. "Lieutenant, I'll give you and your people one week to find out whoever did this and arrest them. After that, I'm stepping into the middle of this case whether you approve of it or not."

The lieutenant was a man in his late forties, a hardened veteran officer who didn't like to be pushed or even mildly threatened. "Marshal Long," he warned, "if you push your nose into this, you could mess up our investigation. If that should happen, you'd find yourself in a shit-load of trouble, so don't even think about getting involved."

"Bob and Emily Muldoon were my close friends. This is personal to me."

"We *all* loved and respected the boss and his wife," the lieutenant said stiffly. "Every man you see in this room wants *blood revenge* . . . but we're doing this investigation slow and careful. And we don't want any interference . . . not even from a federal officer with your sterling reputation."

"One week, Lieutenant," Longarm repeated. "Just find the man or men that did this terrible thing and you'll never see my face getting in your face. Otherwise . . ."

The lieutenant's eyes narrowed. "We've got enough to worry about without any pressure from you, Marshal Long. So stay the hell out of this and let us do our job."

"Sure," Longarm said, looking past the lieutenant and up the hospital corridor. "But do it fast and do it well."

Before the lieutenant could reply, Longarm turned on his heel and headed outside. He perfectly understood the lieutenant's position. Had their roles been reversed, Longarm knew that he would have said exactly the same thing as the officer. But that didn't change the fact that Denver's chief of police and his wife were both fighting for their lives.

Longarm stepped outside into a cold wind that was blowing ice crystals. "Damned endless winter," he muttered as he headed back toward his office wondering how he would handle this investigation if he were in charge of the Denver Police Department.

"Are they still alive?" a young policeman asked as he hurried toward the hospital.

"Yes," Longarm replied. "But just barely."

"Sonofabitch!" the policeman swore. "I hope we can find out who did this and that they hang on a choking rope!"

"We'll find whoever did it," Longarm vowed.

"You bet we will, but it might take some time," the young officer said in a worried voice.

"Officer, you've got one week before I jump in to help."

"What?" The Denver policeman suddenly looked confused.

"One week," Longarm gritted as he headed down the street head bent into the cold, icy wind.

Chapter 3

Longarm had had a long, unproductive week at the office since hearing about his friends being attacked in their own home. The good news was that both Bob and Emily Muldoon were still alive and it was looking as if they would eventually recover from the savage beatings that they'd suffered. The bad news was that both of them would be permanently damaged both in mind and body. The chief was still unconscious and his wife remained deep in shock.

She had been questioned as to the identity of her attacker or attackers, but Longarm had learned through the grapevine that she'd been of little help in furthering the intense investigation. Apparently, she had been jumped from behind and then blindfolded before being beaten and then raped. Police Chief Bob Muldoon had also been caught off guard from behind.

"It looks like the police investigation is going exactly nowhere," Longarm told his boss on an overcast Saturday afternoon just before leaving his office for the weekend.

"How do you know this?"

"I have my information sources inside the police department."

"And you're pretty sure that they're reliable?"

"Completely sure," Longarm said. "I gave notice to them that I'd sit out for a week and that week is up next Monday."

"Custis," Billy warned, "you've got a full-time job right here."

"Things are slow right now," Longarm argued.

"I've got cases that I can send you off on. One in Nevada. One in Arizona. Maybe the best thing for you would be to leave town for a month or so until this thing is wrapped up by the locals."

"They aren't going to 'wrap it up,'" Longarm said with gloom. "I have a gut feeling that whoever did the crime is going to get away with it despite all the manpower that is going into the case."

"You don't know that for sure."

Longarm looked up at his boss. "Billy, I've got a month's vacation time coming."

"Now wait just a minute!" Billy exploded. "If you think I'm going to give you a month off so you can interfere with the local police department's investigation, then you have another think coming."

"You gonna fire me?"

Billy pulled back in surprise. "What is *that* supposed to mean?"

Longarm was on his feet and standing in the middle of the office. "It means exactly what you think it means. I'll quit if you order me to stay in this office and shuffle paperwork while those responsible for nearly killing the Muldoons get away."

"What about going to Nevada or Arizona? You like to travel."

"No," Longarm said flatly. "I'm not going anywhere until the guilty are behind bars or dead in my gun sights."

"You're pushing me into a corner," Billy said, filling his briar pipe.

"No," Longarm argued, "you're the one that's pushing me into a corner. Don't do it, Billy. You know I'll quit this job and turn in my badge if you force the issue."

Billy sighed. "You'd go that far?"

"Damn right."

Billy scratched a match hard and it broke. He scratched another into flame and fired up his pipe, then started puffing fast. "Custis, would you really throw your whole federal career in the shitter over this Muldoon crime?"

"It's a matter of honor," Longarm said without a moment's hesitation. "I'd have no choice."

Billy's normally placid face was now clouded with worry. "Don't you remember that you were warned to stay out of this?"

"And I told them I'd do it . . . for a week. The week is up on Monday, and that's when you'll either let me take vacation time or else I'll hand in my badge and become a civilian."

"You're the stubbornest man I've ever known," Billy groused.

Longarm didn't say a word as he waited for his supervisor's answer.

"Well, dammit!" Billy snapped. "Maybe whoever did it will be caught this weekend."

"I hope so," Longarm told his boss, "but I think that is highly unlikely. So will I get my requested vacation?"

Billy gazed hard at his desktop puffing faster. Finally, he looked up at Longarm and said, "I'm sorry but I just can't have you messing in this case. If my superiors learned of it, then I'd be fired and you'd be fired and what the hell would that accomplish to the good?"

"Nothing," Longarm said. "So I'll make it real easy for you, Billy. I quit."

"No!"

"Yes," Longarm said as he removed his badge. "I'm quitting and you can't stop it. Hire me back when whoever beat the Muldoons half to death and raped Mrs. Muldoon is dead or in jail."

"Dammit!" Billy pounded his desk in frustration. "There must be some other way."

"This is the best way. You've got a fine wife and family. A home and bills to pay for every month. I won't jeopardize that. This will work and you can hire me back when I'm done."

Billy looked devastated. "You're not only my friend, but you're by far the best law officer and detective on my team."

"I'll sign up again . . . provided you don't cut my already pitiful salary," Longarm assured his boss.

"Do you swear to that?"

"I do," Longarm said, sticking out his hand. "And I'll shake on our agreement."

"But it won't go into effect until Monday," Billy said.

"Okay. Monday it is," Longarm agreed. "But the Denver police haven't a lead or a clue so nothing will change."

"You never know." Billy said, sliding Longarm's badge back across his desk. "But if you do quit on me and start working on the case, do you have any idea where to start?"

"I know a few men that would have really carried a hatred for the chief."

"Like who?"

"I'd rather keep that to myself."

"I understand. Just be careful. Someone who would do that to the Muldoons has to be utterly depraved and ruthless."

"I think that there was more than one man involved."

14

"You could be right," Billy said.

Longarm retrieved his badge and then the two federal officers shook hands.

"Monday," Billy reiterated. "You hand it in on Monday. Until then, you're still a federal officer."

"All right," Longarm agreed knowing that on Monday he was going to be a civilian and start his relentless hunt for whoever had committed the assault on his dear old friends. "Monday it is."

Chapter 4

Longarm had a second-story apartment located across from Cherry Creek and the park. It wasn't much of an apartment, just a two-room flat with a bath and commode down at the end of the hallway. But the rent was cheap, no one bothered him, and he was often on the road so he didn't spend any time or money fixing the place up. What he liked about it was that it had a nice window view of Cherry Creek and there were a few saloons that he favored on the same city block.

One of the other things he liked about his humble but safe lodgings was that he wasn't bothered much by the landlady, who was drunk most of the time and only knocked on his door when the rent was overdue. Other than Mrs. Shelton, people left him alone, never questioned his female guests, and were quiet and polite. Most of them knew that he was a federal officer, and that was the reason why the landlady gave him a small discount on his monthly rent.

"If I get a bad tenant in here, you'll throw him out, won't you?" she'd often asked.

"Yes, Mrs. Shelton, I most certainly would encourage them to leave."

"That's what I like to hear, Marshal. This is a fine, upstanding establishment and I want to keep it that way. And by the way, Marshal Long, would you like to come down and share a little of my whiskey tonight?"

Longarm had always declined the invitation because Mrs. Shelton was kind of a physical wreck but still possessed a lusty imagination. Also, when she got into her cups she could talk a man's legs off. Even worse, all she ever talked about were the men that had loved and left her, as well as endlessly gossiping about the other tenants.

And so, when Longarm heard a knock on his door that Saturday evening just as he was about to go out and have some dinner and a few beers, he frowned with impatience. "Mrs. Shelton," he called, "I slipped the rent under your door yesterday morning. It was in a white envelope. Same as always."

"I'm not Mrs. Shelton," a woman said. "I'm Abby McCall and I need to speak to you at once."

Longarm finished combing his hair while trying to think of someone he knew by that name. Failing, he put his hand on the knob and, not wanting to open up to a total stranger, said, "What is this about, Mrs. McCall?"

"It's about the Muldoon case. I'm a good friend of Emily Muldoon and I need to speak to you tonight."

Longarm couldn't remember Emily mentioning an Abby, but he decided to open his door anyway. "Good evening, young lady," he said to a pretty woman in her mid-twenties with blond hair and blue eyes. "What can I do for you?"

"I understand that you and the Muldoons were very close."

18

"Yes."

She looked past him toward the clutter that was typical of his state of affairs. "What I have to say is of a very private nature. May I come in for just a moment, please?"

"Of course." Longarm stepped aside and let the woman come into his abode. "The place is a mess," he told her. "But I'm a lousy housekeeper and wasn't expecting company this evening."

"No matter at all," Abby said, turning to appraise him carefully. "I . . . I thought long and hard about coming here to see you. I've gone back and forth on it and it's rather driving me crazy."

Longarm swept some old newspapers off his only decent sofa chair and motioned the woman to sit, but she shook her head. "I'd rather stand. You appear to be about to leave and I don't want to be a bother."

"I'm in no hurry and I have no one that is expecting to meet me this evening, so please sit and relax. If you have something important to tell me about the crime against our mutual friends, then I don't want you to feel rushed."

"Thank you," she said, sitting down just as a yellow-striped tomcat appeared on Longarm's windowsill. "Oh, is he yours?" the woman asked.

"Tom is his own boss and belongs to no one," Longarm answered. "When I'm in town he comes and goes through my open window. I like his independence and he likes mine. However, usually when I have company, he prefers to stay outside unless he senses that my company likes cats. Do you like cats?"

"Very much," Abby said, visibly relaxing. "And they almost always like me."

Tom proved this to be true by coming over to brush up against her leg and then hop into her lap.

19

"Tom!" Longarm scolded. "You're far too forward and have apparently lost your manners. Mrs. McCall, I think I'll toss Tom out the window for misbehaving."

"Oh, please don't do that. It's a long way to the ground and he might be injured."

"No," Longarm said, "Tom seems to have the ability to land on his feet every time, and the worst that would happen would be that I'd have injured his pride."

Abby petted the tomcat and it purred loudly. Then, the woman looked up at Custis and said, "I'm very, very nervous. I don't suppose you'd have a little whiskey to steady my frazzled nerves?"

"Of course! Sorry."

Longarm always bought high-quality whiskey instead of the rotgut swill you generally found in the low-class saloons. "I'll get you a glass."

"Not too much," Abby said. "I'm just so nervous."

"I understand," Longarm told her, not understanding at all as he poured them both liberal doses of the excellent liquor. "Here you go."

Abby raised her glass and said, "To justice!"

"To justice," he repeated as he pulled a kitchen chair closer and took a seat. "And to the Muldoons . . . may they both have a full and complete recovery and may whoever harmed them strangle at the end of a hangman's noose."

"Hear. Hear!"

Abby McCall drained her glass, and didn't object when Longarm refilled it and then asked, "Now what exactly do you have to tell me?"

She bit her lip, and then whispered as if they were in a room full of eavesdroppers, "I think I *might* know who did it."

Longarm nearly dropped his glass on his littered and unmopped hardwood floor. "Who?"

She took another big swallow. "I'm not sure about this . . . what I tell you is just a strong hunch."

"You just go right ahead and tell me," he said.

"All right then, but you must never reveal this conversation to anyone."

"I wouldn't dream of it."

"Good." She took a deep, steadying breath, then went on. "Marshal Long, I think the one who nearly killed the Muldoons and then violated Emily was a lieutenant in the local police department."

"What?" Longarm was not sure that he had heard the woman correctly.

"A lieutenant," she repeated.

Longarm moved closer to the woman and gazed straight into her eyes. "And his name?"

She turned her gaze down to the floor. "I'd rather not tell you quite yet."

Longarm was puzzled. "Why not?"

"Because, if I give you this man's name, you might get killed or tortured and be forced to tell them about me. In that case, we'd both end up dead!"

Longarm took a deep swallow of his whiskey and decided it would be unwise to press this woman too hard, so he said, "Why don't we start by first you telling me who *you* are."

"I told you my name."

"I know. Abby McCall. And you're not wearing a wedding band, so can I assume you are single?"

"That is true. I worked as a maid and then was soon promoted to a sort of personal secretary and confidante to Mrs. Muldoon before I left their home and employ."

"Then you did rather well for yourself," Longarm said, wanting to say something encouraging to the frightened woman.

21

"I did. I loved Mrs. Muldoon and her husband and was a good and loyal employee for five years. You see, Marshal, the family took me in off the streets, so to speak, and taught me how to dress and act like a lady and then make my way confidently in this world."

"And what do you do today to support yourself?"

"I am the personal secretary of a very rich and retired old gentleman named Milburn Stanton who made his fortune in Colorado mining and lives—"

"I know the man and where he lives," Longarm interrupted. "I heard that Mr. Stanton is on death's doorstep."

"I'm afraid that is true. I would not be surprised if he passes away within the next day or two given his poor physical condition and mental state of mind. Marshal, please do not misunderstand, but his passing would almost be a mercy."

"Then you will soon be unemployed?"

"Mr. Stanton has been taken to the hospital to die. He is unconscious."

"I'm sorry to hear that. And what about you?"

"I am extremely fortunate in that Mr. Stanton has left me a generous amount of money in his will. I am happy to say that I will never have to work for anyone again . . . unless it is of my choosing."

Longarm felt the conversation was drifting too far off the subject of the Muldoons. "I am glad to hear that. But let's get back to the Muldoons. Why do you think that one of the chief's own officers did this terrible thing to him and his wife?"

Abby McCall did not hesitate in her reply. "Because he was passed over by the chief as his eventual replacement."

Longarm raised his eyebrows. "I know the hierarchy of the department quite well. And knowing it, I'd say you'd have to be talking about Lieutenant Gavin Kelly."

She looked up, obviously startled by the accuracy of his guess. "Why, yes," she said, "that is exactly who I suspect committed this atrocity."

Longarm took a deep swallow. "I know Lieutenant Kelly quite well. He was the one that I spoke to at the hospital. I thought him a fine officer and a very upright young man."

"He's a scoundrel and a liar!"

Longarm was shocked by the outpouring of hatred he heard in the young woman's voice. "Miss," he said, "perhaps you have some personal and unhappy involvement with the lieutenant and your judgment might therefore be swayed unfavorably toward this decorated police officer."

She jumped up and slammed her glass down hard on a little table. "Marshal, I see coming here has been a terrible mistake. Please excuse me and forget that I was ever here, much less that I suggested I had any knowledge of who attacked the Muldoon family."

The woman was headed for the door when Longarm overtook her and grabbed her arm. "Now wait just a minute here, Abby."

"Let go of me this instant!"

"Or what? You'll call the police?" Longarm released her arm, but continued to block her path to the closed door. "You're not leaving until we talk this out," he said, putting a slight edge to his voice so that she would know he meant business.

Suddenly, the woman burst into tears. Longarm hated it when women cried, and he was momentarily at a loss what to do. So he just stood in front of his door and waited until she regained her composure. It took a few minutes, but when Abby stopped crying, she sat down and held up her glass for a refill.

"I'm a wreck," she confessed. "You shouldn't listen to a word that I've said or am about to say."

"I'll be the judge of that," Longarm told her. "Now why don't you tell me why you think that Lieutenant Gavin Kelly is the guilty party. And I want you to be specific, factual, and above all truthful. Because you must remember that you are taking aim at a man who has dedicated his career to law enforcement."

"All right," she said, taking another drink and then looking him in the eye. "I am sure that you think I have a personal vendetta against Lieutenant Kelly and you are correct. He promised to marry me and I gave him . . . everything."

"Everything?"

"Yes. Money and . . . well, you can guess. Only later did I learn that he consorts with all manner of prostitutes and is sexually depraved."

"Never mind that," Longarm said impatiently. "Why would the lieutenant commit such an atrocity against the Muldoons? I mean, if he felt wronged by being overlooked for promotion, there would have been official channels in the department where he could address a legitimate grievance."

"You don't know Gavin like I know him," Abby said. "And you don't know that I am the reason that he didn't get that big promotion, because I told Mr. Muldoon and Emily about Gavin's dark side."

"You mean the whores?"

"Yes, and much worse."

"Go on," Longarm said, his eyes narrowing with concentration.

"All right, I'll just spit it out," she decided, emptying her glass and starting to look a little potted. "Lieutenant Gavin Kelly is connected to Denver's criminal kingpins and has murdered under the guise of acting in his official capacity as a police officer. In short, Gavin has been an executioner hiding behind his badge. And when I learned that and told it to the Muldoons, that was the end of Gavin's chance to become police chief."

"If this is true, why wasn't he immediately arrested?"

"No proof," Abby said. "Gavin is very careful and all of his victims are very dead."

Longarm scowled, still wondering if this woman was at all trustworthy. "All right. So you learned of these murders and then told the chief and this caused the lieutenant to try to silence him."

"Yes. And he of course tried to make the crime look like it was done by a criminal with a grudge against the chief."

"Why wouldn't Lieutenant Kelly silence *you*?"

Abby shuddered. "Because he knows that I am going to inherit a great deal of money from the Stanton estate. He has told me privately that I will either turn everything I inherit over to him or he will kill me . . . very slowly."

Abby's eyes brimmed up with tears. "Marshal Long, don't you see that I couldn't go to the local police because it would get back to Gavin and he'd be forced to silence me at once?"

"I suppose I can see that."

"So I had to go outside the department to a stranger. And I picked you because you are a federal officer of the law and are quite famous for your bravery."

Longarm modestly waved that off. "Have you any proof about these murders that you say Lieutenant Kelly committed?"

"No. I don't even know the names of the victims. I just know that Gavin got stinking drunk a few times and bragged about being paid."

Longarm grimaced. "As you probably know, in a court of law it would be your word against the lieutenant's."

"Yes."

"And any judge or jury would side with Lieutenant Kelly."

"Sure they would." Abby sniffled. "So you see, I am damned if I come forward and damned if I don't. Either way, I will be sacrificed. Even now, Gavin is probably searching for me. I would bet my life that he has already been to the Stanton estate and discovered my absence."

"Then you have to go underground until I find out how to bring him down and get enough evidence on the man to pin him to what happened to the Muldoons."

"Where can I run to?"

Longarm considered the question and eliminated all the choices but one. "Did anyone see you come up to this apartment?"

"Not that I know of."

"Then you can stay here while I handle this."

"But—"

"You'll be safe here," Longarm said. "Safer than in a hotel or trying to get on the train to leave town. If what you've told me is true, all of those places will be watched."

She looked around the cluttered apartment. "I don't know."

"I can't force you to stay here, and I can't even promise that you will be completely safe when I am out of this room. But it's the best that I can do for tonight. You can sleep in my bed and I'll sleep on the floor."

"No, I couldn't inconvenience you so."

Longarm shrugged his broad shoulders. "Are you hungry?"

"Famished."

"I'll go down to the store and buy something for us to eat and drink tonight. In the morning, you can go or stay."

"Thank you," she whispered. "Your whiskey is good and it's almost gone."

"I'll get another bottle."

"Marshal Long."

"Custis. Call me Custis."

"Well, Custis, thank you for helping and believing me. I've been honest with you and I'm sure that my life is hanging by a thread. You do believe me, don't you?"

He studied her for a moment and found himself nodding his head. "Yes," he said, "but I'll have to check out your story about being formerly employed by the Muldoons and Mr. Stanton."

"Do that. And then please save me. If you do, I'll be generous. From my inheritance I'll pay whatever price you ask."

"Abby, we'll talk about that soon enough," Longarm promised as he buckled on his gun belt and grabbed his hat before heading out the door. "Double lock this door and don't let anyone in or out except my tomcat until I return."

"I won't," she promised. "Because Gavin is out there right now relentlessly searching for me and he won't rest until I'm a dead woman."

Chapter 5

When Longarm returned to his apartment with groceries and another bottle of good whiskey, he found Abby half-dressed with Tom curled up and purring in her arms.

"I love this cat! Are you sure that others feed him when you're away?"

"They must because he survives for weeks at a time in my absence," Longarm replied as he set the groceries on the table. "I hope you like ham and cheese sandwiches."

"I do."

"I even bought some red wine to wash them down with. And the makings for a good breakfast tomorrow morning."

"You are very kind. I have some money in my purse and I'll repay you."

He waved that off. "Don't worry about it. And thanks for straightening up the place. I don't know how you did it so quickly."

"You were gone for forty-five minutes. I was afraid that . . ."

He looked at her. "That what? That I might betray you because I think you're lying?"

"Something like that," she admitted.

"I wouldn't do that," he said. "I'll find out tomorrow if what you've told me so far is true."

"Even about the lieutenant?"

"I'll find out if he likes prostitutes. I know a few and they talk a lot with very few secrets. If the lieutenant has been consorting with them and has some strange urges, I'll learn about them."

Abby actually blushed. "Well, that's not so important . . . at least it shouldn't be as far as the Muldoons are concerned, but you'll find out that he does have a dark side and is sexually depraved."

As she said this, Abby's cheeks colored. "I guess you must think very little of me for having . . . having gone along with his carnal depravities."

"I'm not going to judge anyone about what they do in the privacy of their bedroom," Longarm said quietly. "Because I've probably done the same thing more than once."

Her eyes widened. "Oh, I don't think you have, Marshal."

"Custis. Remember?"

"Sorry."

"Here," he said, unpacking the groceries and laying them on the table. "Fix us a couple of sandwiches and open the wine. I'm going down to the end of the hall and take a bath. It's been a long day."

"Please hurry back."

Longarm turned and looked at the woman. She appeared to be a little drunk, a lot scared, and somehow still very desirable. "I will, Abby."

She came up to him and kissed his cheek. "I'm ashamed of what I did with Gavin, but I thought we were in love and therefore it was all right."

"I don't need to know a thing."

"Thank you," she whispered as she kissed his lips and then went to make them a quick supper.

• • •

It was midnight when they finished the wine and together went to his bed at her insistence. Both now fully undressed, she hugged him tightly and whispered in Longarm's ear, "Without you I'm a dead woman."

"I think that's an exaggeration."

"I don't. Gavin is cunning. He told me that he pulled every string and even used blackmail to leapfrog over the other officers and get promoted to lieutenant. If you think he'll be easy to pin this crime on, you are wrong."

"Did he actually say that he attacked the Muldoons?"

"Not in so many words. But it was clear from what he said between the lines."

"Did he ever mention the names of these criminals that he consorts with?"

"No."

Longarm's brows furrowed. "Abby, if push comes to shove, I may have to use you as *bait*."

He felt her stiffen beside him in the bed. "What do you mean!"

"I'll investigate his background this weekend. I'm sure that I'll find out that Lieutenant Kelly has consorted with prostitutes, but that's not a crime and it certainly wouldn't tie him to what happened to the Muldoon family."

"But—"

"Let me finish," Longarm said. "If worse does come to worst, you can contact him and tell him you'll pay him all your newly gotten inheritance money. I'll be listening in the next room along with someone whose testimony will stand up in court. We can get him on extortion, and if you can get him to admit that he was the attacker, we can put him in prison and maybe even send him to the gallows."

Abby didn't say a word. She just shivered with fright. Longarm rolled over and held her tightly. "Don't worry. I

31

can probably think of an easier way. What I've just told you would be used only as a last resort."

"I hope so," she whispered, kissing his face and then sliding her hand down to his manhood. "But can we stop talking about this for tonight? I'm scared enough without the thought of having to face Gavin Kelly ever again. Just . . . just hold me tight and make me forget everything except you and me and that peeping tomcat staring at us from your windowsill."

"Is he watching *again*?" Longarm asked, raising up on his elbow and seeing Tom's glittering green eyes reflected in the streetlamp below. "Yes, he is, the furry little pervert."

"I don't care if Tom is watching or not," Abby said, tossing the bedsheet aside so that they were completely uncovered and unencumbered. "I like to start out on top. How about you?"

Longarm grinned into the semidarkness. "I don't care where you start as long as I get to finish."

For the first time, Abby giggled, and it had a nice, girlish sound. She sat up on her knees, took his manhood in her hands, and began to massage it up and down until it was standing tall and proud.

"It's huge," she said, bending over and licking the top of his rod with her tongue. "It's like a giant cobra."

"Have you ever even seen a cobra?"

"I sure have," she told him. "I saw one in a circus, and it stood right up and waved back and forth in front of an Indian snake charmer. I couldn't take my eyes off that cobra."

Longarm chuckled. "Well, that's the first time I ever heard it compared to a cobra. The thing you need to know, Abby, is that my cobra doesn't bite. It just spits."

Abby bent low and took him in her mouth, and then began to work him up and down until Longarm groaned with pleasure. "Girl, you're *drowning* that big snake," he protested in jest.

"And now I'm going to *suffocate* it in the nicest way imaginable," she said, rising up and then lowering herself slowly until Longarm was completely sheathed inside her. "So how does it like this?"

"It likes it fine," he said, a growl deep in his throat as he took Abby by the hips and began to move her tight little bottom up and down.

"Is your cobra ready to spit yet?" she moaned much later.

"No. He can hold his breath a long time."

"Oh," she whispered, bending over so that he could suck on her nipples. "This is very nice."

Longarm thought so too. And because they were both a little drunk, it was going to take quite some time to drown his big snake in her juices. So he let the big boy die slow and happy as their hips began to move faster and faster.

When the fire in his loins was finally at a melting point, Longarm rolled Abby onto her back and began to slam his snake deeper and deeper until the woman was crazy with desire and then crying out with ecstasy and her entire body was shuddering with release.

"Oh, Marshal," she gasped, throwing her head back. "Give it to me right now! Spit! Spit!"

Longarm's big cobra spit seed and he filled Abby until she overflowed. Then, with a sigh of contentment, he slumped forward every bit as limp as a neck-wrung rooster.

And from the sill Tom howled and then sailed straight out the window to land on a tree limb not far below. Longarm smiled because that tomcat was almost certainly going off to find his own hot little hole to ride.

Chapter 6

Longarm slept fitfully that night beside Abby, and awoke shortly after dawn feeling tired and a little thickheaded. He shaved, then dressed, and was about to leave the apartment when Abby awoke with a start.

"Are you leaving already?" she asked with obvious concern.

"Yes. I'll be gone all day talking to police officers who know and have worked with Lieutenant Kelly."

"They are thicker than fleas," Abby said. "You won't get one officer to say a bad word about another."

"You might be surprised," Longarm replied. "If what you said about Kelly using underhanded and even criminal means to get his promotion is true, then he's bound to have made some lasting enemies in the department."

"But if that were the case, wouldn't their testimony be tainted by their hatred of the man?"

"I'm sure it would be," Longarm replied. "But I'm not looking for someone to testify in court against the lieutenant. And also, there are some women who will know if Kelly has a bad or sadistic streak. Such things can't be kept a secret even in a town as big as Denver."

"Be careful," she urged, coming out of bed and giving Longarm a hug. "If Gavin finds out you are out to get him, he'll do everything he can to have you silenced. And with you gone, I'm a walking dead woman."

Longarm kissed Abby on the forehead. "Now be honest. Who are you more concerned about here?"

"Myself," she admitted. "I know that that sounds shameless, but I don't want to be tortured and I do want to live long enough inherit the money that Mr. Stanton has so generously left me in his will. Is that so terrible?"

"No," Longarm told her, "and it's refreshingly truthful. If you'd have said anything else, I've have known you were lying."

"I haven't lied to you about anything. Not even my sordid past."

"Forget the past and let's see if we can make sure you have a bright and prosperous future."

"Custis, if I do . . . I mean, if you stop Lieutenant Gavin Kelly once and for all . . . I'll make sure you're well paid."

"You don't have to say that. I'm just doing my job."

"But it isn't you job . . . is it? I mean, this is a local matter and you're a federal officer. You don't have to become involved."

"Sure I do," he said, deciding not to tell her that he would be resigning on Monday and turning in his badge so that he could bring whoever attacked the Muldoons to justice.

Longarm left Abby standing at the door looking apprehensive. He waited in the hallway until he heard her turn the dead bolt from inside, and then he went downstairs and out into the street.

A good hearty breakfast, he thought. *And plenty of coffee to sweep away the cobwebs from my brain before I set about to find out if Abby has told me the complete truth.*

• • •

He'd had a good breakfast and about four cups of coffee strong enough to make him feel almost human. Longarm wasn't looking forward to his work this day, and he bore a frown on his face as he trudge up the street heading for the red-light district of town. If it was true that the lieutenant was as crooked as a snake in a cactus patch and as cunning as a hungry coyote, then he would not be an easy man to bring down.

Kelly would have covered his tracks with layers of corruption, and he'd have greased a lot of dirty palms in order to keep his secrets well hidden. In short, Longarm knew that getting to the truth of who Lieutenant Kelly was would be difficult and dangerous. Prostitutes would know Kelly was a monster, but they tended to be just as much of a closemouthed society as policemen . . . usually out of a well-justified sense of self-preservation.

"I'll talk to The Gypsy first," Longarm decided aloud. "She knows every dark and dirty secret in Denver society."

No one knew The Gypsy's real name or even if she was a true Gypsy. No one knew her age or her background or if she had a family or had ever cried or lost a love. What was known about The Gypsy was that she was middle-aged and still stunningly beautiful with masses of black ringlets and a voluptuous figure that had defied both time and gravity.

The Gypsy was also very rich and powerful. She was the kind of remarkable person who had a mysterious background and attracted men of power and position rather than repelled them. She was always dressed in the latest fashions from Paris, and wore at least a pound of pure gold and precious stones. The Gypsy preferred sapphires, but she also liked diamonds and rubies . . . lots of them, and only those that were of great size and value. She counted almost all of Denver's most powerful politicians as her friends, and once a year she toured Europe visiting nobility, which made her the envy of wealthy and influential women.

Longarm knew that The Gypsy was known to consort with Denver's most successful artisans and courtesans and was very generous in her gifts to charity. On her darker side, some whispered that The Gypsy was addicted to opium, but Longarm did not believe it for a moment. Others said she was not a noblewoman, but a witch from Romania who had poisoned her fabulously wealthy old husband in favor of a much younger lover.

Longarm didn't know anything about The Gypsy's past nor did he care. He had made her acquaintance at a horse auction where they had both bid on an especially fine stallion. The Gypsy, of course, had easily outbid Longarm, but then had graciously offered to let him ride the horse whenever he wished. That had led to a friendship that had never quite blossomed into a passionate affair . . . but they both expected that to happen in the not-too-distant future. In the meantime, they had simply enjoyed each other's company while horseback riding in the foothills above Denver.

And now, as Longarm knocked on the front door to her elegant mansion, he wondered if The Gypsy would really know the secrets of a man with no more official standing than a mere police lieutenant.

"Marshal Long, come in," the maid said with a bow and a smile. "Are you here to see Madame Reneau?"

"If my sudden appearance is not an imposition to the lady."

"I will ask her. Please come inside and make yourself comfortable."

Longarm removed his flat-brimmed Stetson and wiped the dirt from his boots on the doorstep rug before entering the great foyer with its marble-lined walls and high alabaster ceilings. On the walls was some of the finest artwork in Denver, which he admired while waiting for The Gypsy.

He did not have long to wait.

This woman knew how to make an entrance . . . that was for certain. She came floating down a spiral staircase as if she was being transported on a warm wind. When The Gypsy landed at the foot, she was smiling graciously, and in the soft light of the hallway Longarm thought she might be perhaps the most elegant woman he had ever beheld.

"Custis! What a pleasure it is to have you visit."

"My pleasure," he assured The Gypsy. "And might I say that you look as ravishing as always?"

"Of course you might say that!" The Gypsy fluttered her long lashes and her cheeks colored with pleasure at the compliment. "But if I were all that ravishing in your eyes, you handsome devil, why have you *not yet seduced me*?"

Longarm was momentarily caught without words. The Gypsy had the talent to do that, and he suspected that she did it to amuse herself. "Well, my dear," he said, trying to recover, "very soon I might strive to rectify that sad omission."

"I do hope so, my dear Marshal Long," she said looking straight into his eyes. "Can you stay for champagne and the excellent chamber music that I have scheduled for a ladies' luncheon? Although I have to say that you would no doubt be a major distraction from the music."

"I'm afraid I'll have to decline," he said, trying to look disappointed. "Actually, I have a serious matter to discuss with you concerning someone of limited but growing influence that you might know . . . or at least have heard of."

The Gypsy's eyebrows arched. "If this person has any influence at all, then I will certainly know them. Would you like to join me in the library where we could talk in comfort?"

"I would."

Longarm followed The Gypsy into a library that was larger than the entire upstairs of his apartment building. Books lined massive mahogany cases from floor to ceiling, and yet Longarm had the feeling that none of them had even been opened . . . much less read. The Gypsy was not a scholar; she was far too engaged in the business of living her own fascinating story.

Longarm waited until she was seated before he sank into a deep leather chair and then leaned forward and began. "I don't have much time. There are lives in danger."

"Does this concern Mr. and Mrs. Muldoon?"

"It does," Longarm admitted, impressed by her perception.

"What an abominable act of cowardice and savagery! Do you know who did this thing to those kind old people?"

"Perhaps," he said. "I do have a suspect. Or at least I have someone that has been pointed out to me that would have cause to do Chief Muldoon harm."

The Gypsy's eyelids drooped slightly. "And that is why you are here? To ask me if I know of this . . . this person?"

"Exactly."

"Give me his name."

"His name is Lieutenant Gavin Kelly."

Her eyes widened with surprise. "A police officer!"

"Yes."

"And a lieutenant?"

"I'm afraid so."

"I don't know him," she said. "I'm very sorry, but Mr. Kelly would be beneath the level of men that I associate or come into contact with. I would have thought you would have known that yourself, Custis."

"I'm only a marshal," he said, pointing out the fact. "And this man is a lieutenant. Yet you and I are friends."

"Good point," she conceded. "But the difference is that you are both devastatingly handsome as well as famous . . . as famous as Buffalo Bill Cody."

"Hardly. My dear woman, you flatter me far too much."

"We flatter each other shamelessly and what is the harm? But anyway, about this person named Lieutenant Gavin Kelly. What do you really want to know about him?"

Longarm quickly told The Gypsy what Abby had told him the night before. He ended by saying, "And if Lieutenant Kelly does have such an unsavory background with prostitutes, then that would be the reason for him being denied further promotion in the department."

"If the rumor is true about him," The Gypsy pointed out.

"Yes, if it is true. Could you find out? I need to know if this decorated police officer has a dark side . . . one dark enough that he would take revenge not only on our police chief, but also his poor wife."

"I will find out the truth about this man. But why would this lieutenant do such a terrible thing to Mrs. Muldoon?"

Longarm steepled his fingers together and gathered his thoughts before he finally replied, "I have asked myself the same question. If Kelly so hated the chief . . . why hurt his poor wife? Where is the gain or the reason? And do you know the answer that I keep coming up with?"

The Gypsy stared at him with rapt attention. "No. By all means you must tell me."

"If Lieutenant Kelly did rape and outrage Mrs. Muldoon, then it was only to throw the investigation a red herring. To send them down the wrong path and make the investigators assume that the perpetrator was some half-crazed ex-convict that was just out to get even and make Chief Muldoon pay by hurting not only him . . . but also the very thing that he most loved . . . his wife."

The Gypsy sighed. "Sadly, I do see what you mean. How diabolical and devious that would make Lieutenant Kelly."

"Yes, it would. But my theory only holds water if this man has a flawed nature and dark past."

"I have a dark past, my dear marshal." She managed a smile. "But I would never savage innocent people."

"But this is different," Longarm argued. "We are talking about a man who has been a police officer long enough to have seen the worst of the worst in mankind and perhaps has taken on that mold. A man that will stop at absolutely nothing to gain power. A man that desperately desires to be the next police chief and will let nothing stand in the way of that goal."

The Gypsy nodded with understanding. "So what you want me to do is to find out what kind of a man this Lieutenant Kelly *really* is."

"Yes. And I need to know the truth about him in a hurry. I'll be talking to some people who might help me with answers, but the very fact that I carry a federal officer's badge will be a barrier to my getting the truth."

"I'll find out what you need to know immediately," The Gypsy promised. "As soon as my luncheon is over. It is to raise money for the local hospital expansion, you know. It's a very important need for Denver."

"I'm sure it is. And I thank you."

"Can you come by to see me this evening?" The Gypsy asked. "If Lieutenant Gavin Kelly has any skeletons in his closet, I'll know about them by then."

"I'll be by."

"This Abby that you mentioned and who worked for Mr. Stanton . . . I know her."

"You do?"

"Yes. Mr. Stanton is my friend. I understand he is dying."

"I'm afraid so."

"And I suspect that Abby is a benefactor in his will."

"She admitted that she was and that the amount of money she will receive is substantial."

"Do you trust her as much as you trust me?" The Gypsy asked bluntly.

Longarm was caught off guard. "Why do you ask?"

"I just wonder if she is telling the truth or if she might have some part in the dark side of this crime."

Longarm took a deep breath. "If she is to inherit a great deal of money from Mr. Stanton in the very near future . . . then why would she have anything to do with someone like the lieutenant?"

"You said she already was involved with him."

"But no more. In fact, Lieutenant Kelly has threatened to torture and kill Abby if she doesn't turn over all of her Stanton inheritance money."

"So she tells you, Marshal. So she tells you."

"But—"

"Just be careful," The Gypsy said. "I'm not saying the girl has anything to do with this intrigue . . . but then again she might. And if she were involved, it would be your life that is in the most immediate danger."

Longarm nodded with understanding. He did not for a minute believe that Abby had told him anything but the complete truth . . . and yet The Gypsy was right. He hardly knew Abby, and he'd already dipped his wick in her. Something like that could temporarily cause a man to lose his best judgment.

Anyway, The Gypsy's words were always worth careful consideration, and he would keep this warning to be on guard with Abby well in mind.

"Tonight at eight," he said.

"And please don't come smelling like Abby."

"Why would you say that?" he asked.

"Because whatever I have to tell you need not be tainted by lust, but instead by cold reason."

Longarm did not know what kind of response he could give to that. But maybe . . . just maybe . . . The Gypsy knew a thing or two about Abby that she wasn't ready to reveal.

Then again, maybe she was just a shade jealous. It would be interesting to find out one way or the other.

Chapter 7

Longarm spent the day asking discreet questions about Lieutenant Kelly and getting mixed answers. Several prostitutes hinted that Kelly was twisted and a sadist, but none would come right out and say that and give Longarm specifics. One, a redhead named Flora, just threw up her hands when Longarm pressed her and said, "Kelly is a powerful policeman and I ain't sayin' nothin' to nobody against him. 'Cause, if I did, I might wind up facedown in Cherry Creek."

"No one would hurt you, Flora. And I wouldn't let on about anything you told me about the lieutenant."

"I believe you, Marshal Long. Honest I do! But I just can't talk about no policeman unless it's to say somethin' nice."

"And you can't say anything nice about Lieutenant Kelly?"

"Well, he's sure a good-lookin' man," Flora finally said. "Not as handsome as you are, but good-lookin' all the same."

"And that's it?"

"Yes, sir. That's it. I am shuttin' my big mouth so that I can go on livin' and workin' in this town."

Longarm was exasperated by his conversation not only with Flora, but with the other prostitutes he tried to talk to about Lieutenant Kelly. The only thing that was obvious was that it took no more than the lieutenant's name to strike fear into the hearts of these women. And that meant that Kelly did have a very dark and dangerous side. Even so, that wasn't nearly enough to tie the police officer into the crimes against Chief Muldoon and his wife.

Longarm was too discouraged to go back to his apartment at the end of the day, and so he ate alone knowing that there was plenty of food in his apartment for Abby. She'd be upset that he hadn't come back since leaving early in the morning, but Longarm wanted to see The Gypsy again.

And so, promptly at eight o'clock, he arrived back at her door. He was not in a good mood and when he saw The Gypsy's face, his spirits didn't improve.

Longarm said, "I can tell by your expression that you've learned something about Kelly and it's not gonna qualify him for sainthood."

"You can say that again," The Gypsy answered. "Want a drink?"

"Yes," he answered.

"How about a strong glass of excellent French brandy?"

"I'd prefer whiskey."

"Actually," she said, "so would I. Let's take it in the library. The maid has retired and we can speak freely."

"What do you have to say that is so damaging to Lieutenant Kelly?"

"We'll get to that in a moment."

Longarm followed The Gypsy into her library and she

46

pushed a button that caused one of the tall bookshelves to revolve in a half circle, turning it into a well-stocked bar.

"Nice," Longarm said, quite impressed. "It's always interesting to see how the rich live."

"We live very well," The Gypsy told him. "But it isn't all peaches and cream. We have our own unique set of problems."

"Oh, really?" he asked as she poured them each three fingers of the finest whiskey that could be bought. "And what would they be . . . without getting too specific?"

"When you don't have much or any money . . . you worry about getting it. When you have a lot of money, you worry about how to keep it. Sometimes, how to keep it is even more bedeviling than getting it."

"I doubt that."

"It's true. When you have money, you never know who your true friends are. Most of the people that you come in contact with are after something rather than just the pleasure of your company."

"*I'm* after something," Longarm said. "But it's information about Lieutenant Kelly instead of your money."

"I know. You very badly want to know what I've found out about Lieutenant Gavin Kelly. One part of you hopes that he has a past that will allow you to trap and arrest him . . . but the other part of you hopes that because he's an officer of the law he's squeaky-clean."

"That's right. And then there is Miss Abby McCall. Your warning has caused me some concern."

"As well it should," The Gypsy told him. "Are you aware that she was a prostitute in New York City, Richmond, Chicago, and Omaha before she was chased out of those towns and wound up here in Denver, where she immediately jumped back into her well-practiced profession?"

"She told me she was a former prostitute," Longarm said trying to hide his annoyance. "But also that she'd given up on that profession and improved herself by dint of hard work and good service to her employers."

The Gypsy looked amused. "Let's just say that Miss McCall was more than a housemaid to old Milburn Stanton. Much more."

"I don't care about that," Longarm said dismissively. "Abby wouldn't be the first young woman to sleep with an old man in the hope of inheriting money. And, if she served him well and made him happy . . . and if he was of sound mind when he wrote her into his will . . . then that was his business and his business alone."

The Gypsy listened without interruption and then said, "Are you through defending this young woman that you've obviously bedded and taken under your strong protection?"

"I guess so."

"Well," she said, "then I have to ask you a simple question. Did Abby tell you how much money she is being left in Mr. Stanton's will?"

"Only that it was a sizable and very generous amount."

"Try *all* of his estate. *Every last dime.* And that would, I have been told by reliable sources, be worth over four hundred thousand dollars."

Longarm's jaw dropped. "Cash and stocks?"

"Yes. On top of which, she gets the mansion and its furniture, which is worth another small fortune . . . especially the art collection." The Gypsy raised her glass to Longarm. "I think we should toast to the industry of Miss Abby McCall and to her great good fortune."

The Gypsy's voice was mocking, and Longarm did not join her in the toast because he was stunned by the amount of money that Abby was about to inherit.

"You look shocked, Custis. Perhaps I should have told you this information in a more leisurely manner."

"That's all right. And I *am* shocked."

"Well, my handsome fellow, take a deep drink because I am not quite finished telling you about Miss McCall . . . and by the way, I'm quite sure that is not her real name."

Longarm tossed down his drink, and the fiery whiskey burned all the way down his gullet to his gut. "Let's hear the last of it," he said, feeling greatly disappointed.

"All right. I happen to be very well connected with the people at the hospital where Mr. Stanton is dying. Specifically, Dr. Melvin, the chief of staff and Mr. Stanton's attending physician."

"You went to the hospital room and saw Mr. Stanton?" Longarm asked with surprise.

"No," she replied. "There was no reason to do that. The poor old gentleman is past reason or conversation. He is comatose and slipping away very quickly. I sent someone I trust with a note to Dr. Melvin with a few questions relating to the exact cause of the impending death."

"Old age," Longarm said. "The gentleman must be well into his nineties."

"Ninety-three to be exact. And until he employed Miss McCall, he was in remarkably good health."

"Now wait a minute," Longarm protested, raising his hand. "Surely you're not suggesting that Abby had something to do with his rapid physical decline."

"I'm not suggesting anything of the sort. Dr. Melvin is."

"What!" Longarm almost dropped his glass.

"Dr. Melvin suspects *poisoning*."

"That's . . . that's impossible!" Longarm thundered.

"No," The Gypsy said, "it is not. The only unanswered question is . . . what kind of poison? They've ruled out ar-

49

senic, nor is it any poison that has ever been used commonly in murder. We might never know what poor old Stanton has been given . . . only that it and not age is behind his impending death."

Longarm came to his feet. "What you're saying is that Dr. Melvin only suspects, but can't prove, poisoning."

"That's right."

"Then you've given me nothing. All I've gotten so far on this case concerning Lieutenant Kelly and Miss McCall is theories and speculation. Accusations without a shred of proof."

"Not quite so," The Gypsy said, refilling both of their glasses. "I have some proof that you should find *very* interesting. A very strong connection between Lieutenant Kelly and Miss McCall."

"Let's hear it."

"Why don't I show it to you instead?" the woman suggested, rising up and going to a small desk, where she unlocked a little cabinet and retrieved a paper, which she then gave to Longarm.

He stared in disbelief. "It's a copy of their marriage certificate!"

"Yes," The Gypsy said, "and there is no public record of a divorce. So you see, Miss McCall is really Mrs. Kelly."

"Sonofabitch!" Longarm whispered.

The Gypsy stood up and walked around the library. "I'm sorry that I've distressed you and caused you disappointment. But the moment you told me the woman's name, I knew something about her past, and needed only to check my sources to make sure that I was not prematurely judging her in a bad light. What you have bedded, Custis, is probably a murderess about to inherit more money than you will honestly earn in your entire lifetime. And she is married to the man that she is accusing of another crime."

Longarm had to take a chair. "But why?"

"Who knows?" The Gypsy said with a shrug of her lovely bare shoulders. "I have found out all I can for you. I have done you a great favor. And now, I have one to ask in return."

Longarm was still holding the marriage certificate in his hands and staring at it, but now he glanced up. "Whatever you ask that I can give you," he said. "You've saved me from being a complete and total fool."

"I ask that you make love to me whenever I wish for the next year."

"What!" Longarm couldn't believe what he'd just been told.

She laughed at his shock. "I promise you that it won't be much of an imposition, Custis. And I never misuse a man that I like and admire. And I do admire you."

Recovering a bit, he said, "In spite of my quite obviously being a trusting idiot?"

"Yes, in spite of that. Or maybe because of it. You are chivalrous, Custis, a true Southern gentleman to the core. And so your misjudgment in this matter is not only understandable to me, but it is also admirable."

Longarm took a drink. "We've been friends for what . . . five years?"

"Three and a half," she corrected.

"And we've never been lovers, and maybe that's why we've always liked each other so much."

"I've thought about that a great deal," she admitted. "I've thought about it for two and a half years at least. And while it may be true, I simply no longer care. I want you, Marshal Long. And I think, if you are honest, you have always wanted me."

"I have," he confessed, throwing up his hands. "But right now, the way I'm feeling so much the fool . . . I don't think. . . ."

"Then *don't* think," she told him, setting down her glass and removing his own from his hand. "Just come upstairs and stop thinking. I am going to clear your mind and reinvigorate your body and then you can leave and go about solving this deadly puzzle."

Longarm nodded and stopped thinking. He followed her upstairs still stunned by the news that Abby was married to Kelly. Oh, the hell with it! The Gypsy was right. Maybe it was time to give his mind a momentary rest and let his body take control.

Chapter 8

"It's almost midnight and I've got to go," Longarm said to The Gypsy as he stared up at the ceiling over her bed. "Besides that, I'm nearly exhausted."

She leaned on one elbow and kissed his cheek. "Let's do each other just one more time and I'll let you go home."

Longarm really hadn't had any solid food since breakfast and he was feeling a shade weak. "But . . ."

"Don't worry. I'll do all the work."

There was no arguing with or denying this woman, so Longarm said, "My dear, if you can wring something more out of my carrot, then go ahead and give him more dunking."

The Gypsy slid down Longarm's length, kissing as she moved lower. When she took him in her mouth, he sighed with pleasure and closed his eyes wondering if The Gypsy would be able to get his manhood to stand up one last time this evening.

Longarm didn't have to wait but a few moments and then the woman laughed lustily and cried, "Bravo!"

She climbed on licking her lips with desire. "Since this

is to be our last tonight, I want it to be very slow and utterly delicious."

"I thought the three times we did it already were pretty slow and delicious."

"Not as slow as this will be," she vowed. "It's eleven-thirty now. We'll make this lovemaking last until twelve o'clock."

"You'll get no argument from me," Longarm said, reaching down and running his hands over her buttocks. "No argument at all."

"When you leave here tonight, you won't be in lust and you'll be able to see though Miss McCall's treachery."

Longarm's eyes blinked open. "Is that why we're doing this over and over?"

"Of course not," she said, her hips moving on his well-lubricated rod. "But I want you to sleep well tonight so that your head is clear in the morning. And don't forget that you are going to be my sex slave for the next year. You'll come whenever I feel the urge for you inside of me."

"I'm resigning from the feds soon," he said, wanting to change the subject. "I'm turning in my officer's badge so that I can devote all my time to bringing whoever hurt and almost killed the Muldoons to justice."

"Please *don't* do that!"

Surprised by the passion of her request, Longarm pushed The Gypsy away and said, "Why not? Why do you care?"

"It would be a terrible, perhaps even deadly, mistake."

"I don't think so," Longarm argued. "My boss has already told me that I can't compete in this investigation with the local police. He just doesn't want the federal government to butt into the investigation. That's why I'm resigning."

"Give it a few more days before you resign and justice

will have been served," she told him. "Just three or four more days."

Longarm frowned. "You sound pretty certain of that."

"I am. And you'll be safer in the days to come with your federal officer's badge and authority. Much safer."

"I'll take that under consideration," he promised.

"Good. Now let's not let business spoil the last of this evening's pleasure," she told him as her hips began to move in an ellipse that made Longarm groan. "I might not be able to last until midnight."

"Me neither," she said, inserting her wet tongue into his ear and moving her hips just a little faster.

When he returned to his apartment, it was past one o'clock in the morning, but Abby was wide awake and sitting in his only easy chair waiting impatiently for his return.

"Where have you been?" she demanded, jumping up and marching across the room to confront him.

"I've been investigating," he said, knowing his words sounded false and hollow.

"Investigating *what*! You reek of cheap perfume."

"Actually," he said, "it's very expensive perfume."

"So you have been with a woman all evening while I've been worried sick about you."

"Abby," Longarm said, grabbing her by the shoulders and pushing her out of his face, "don't give me a hard time. We're not married, engaged, or even loosely committed to each other. And I don't appreciate being challenged in my own apartment by a woman that I only met yesterday."

"Who was she?"

"It's none of your business, Abby."

"It *is* my business! My life depends on how discreet you're being in this case."

"Maybe you ought to just leave," Longarm told her

wearily. "I'm tired and out of sorts. And I'll be damned if I'm going to stand here arguing with you into the night."

Abby started to protest, but Longarm just walked around her and began to undress. There was a pitcher of cool water on the counter with a washbasin and a glass. Longarm was thirsty until he remembered that The Gypsy had suggested that Abby might have poisoned poor old Mr. Stanton. With that in mind, he declined a drink of water.

Tomorrow, he would find out the answer to a lot of questions both from Abby herself and from The Gypsy. But tonight, he could definitely feel her eyes boring holes in his backside, and he didn't care as he climbed into bed and promptly fell asleep.

Chapter 9

Longarm awoke early the next morning thinking he was going to his federal office, and then remembered that he'd told his boss that he would be turning in his badge this day.

Should he? Or should he wait three or four more days as The Gypsy had asked? Longarm decided that he probably should wait. He stretched and slipped out of bed, discovering that Abby wasn't lying beside him. Perhaps she was down the hall using the toilet or taking a hot bath.

Longarm dressed and brewed a cup of coffee while waiting for Abby, and he finally grew impatient and went down the hall to the bathroom. Leaning close to the door, he said, "Hey, Abby, we need to talk. What's taking you so long this morning?"

There was no answer. And when he turned the doorknob, there was no Abby inside.

Longarm was instantly concerned. He remembered the confrontation he'd had with Abby last night, and decided she had gotten mad and taken off in a huff. That was a problem because she could be in mortal danger from Lieutenant Gavin Kelly.

Longarm tossed down his coffee and strapped on his

sidearm, which was a Colt Model T that he wore on his left hip butt forward. He then reached for his Ingersoll watch and gold chain. Long ago he had attached a twin-barreled derringer where the watch fob ought to be located. The derringer was a deadly little .44-caliber, and it had saved Longarm's life more than once when he'd acted as if he were checking the time, but instead had produced the little close-quarters pistol.

At the hat stand beside his door, Longarm grabbed his snuff brown Stetson with the crown telescoped flat on top, and then he headed outside. He paused in the hallway and considered leaving his apartment unlocked so that, if Abby should return, she would have a safe place to stay. But he decided against that and locked the door. Longarm was just about to leave when he saw a note on the floor with his name scribbled on the outside.

It read:

Dear Custis. I am sorry we had a fight last evening and I did not sleep a wink. I have decided to return to the Stanton Mansion. I have a gun there in case Lieutenant Kelly comes after me, so don't worry even though I am not sure I could fire on another human in self-defense.

Thank you for your help and, if you can, offer a little prayer for my life.

Abby

"Keerist!" Longarm muttered. "The Stanton Mansion is the *last* place she should be going. Kelly will find and kill her there for sure."

Longarm took off down the stairs on the run. He sprinted

a block, and then hailed a carriage telling the driver to go to Maple Street, where the Stanton Mansion was located, in Denver's most exclusive residential area. "And put some speed on, if you please, driver!"

The driver gave his old dapple-gray horse a sharp swat on the rump, but the animal was stiff in the limbs from all the years of walking on hard cobblestones, and it couldn't pull the carriage much faster than Longarm could have walked. So he fretted as the carriage made its maddeningly slow progress all the way across town. There was a good deal of sewer repair work being done downtown, and that slowed them up another quarter hour. By the time the carriage finally arrived in front of the Stanton Mansion, Longarm was nearly fit to be tied.

"Sorry it took so long," the carriage driver apologized. "Old Dobbin here is twenty-three years old and we've been together for almost fifteen years. He's strong and willing, but like me, he's just not up to a fast pace anymore."

"That's all right," Longarm said, paying the driver and even giving him a nice tip.

"That's some mansion! You want me to wait out here for you, mister?"

"No, thanks."

The carriage driver nodded looking disappointed. "I don't often get customers that come up into this rich neck of the woods. You live here?"

"No," Longarm called over his shoulder. "Just visiting."

Longarm hurried up the long stone pathway that led to the Stanton Mansion, and he didn't bother to knock at the door because he heard angry shouting from inside. One of the voices belonged to Abby and the other, he guessed, was that of Lieutenant Kelly.

Longarm drew his sidearm and burst through the front

door just as shots rang out deep inside the palatial mansion. He raced down the hallway with his Colt in his fist, and heard two more shots followed by a piercing scream.

"Abby!"

Longarm charged into a large dining room and saw Abby lying on the floor beside a big police officer in uniform, Gavin Kelly. "Abby!" he shouted, rushing over to kneel by her side.

She was out cold, but a quick search did not turn up any bullet wounds on the woman's body. Twisting around to stare at the motionless lieutenant, Longarm saw a pool of blood forming under the policeman, who was lying spread-eagled and facedown on a magnificent Persian carpet.

"Shit!" he groused, easing Abby down and rolling Kelly over to stare at the officer's face.

The Denver police lieutenant had been shot at least three times in the chest and stomach, and yet he was still alive, although barely. Longarm took the man's pulse and it was very weak. He knelt and cradled the dying man's head on his knee. "Hang on, Lieutenant," he urged. "I'll go find a doctor."

But the big Irish police officer shook his head and his eyes fluttered open. "Too late. Too late," he whispered, his voice gravelly and filled with an infinite sadness and confusion. "Abby . . ."

"She's alive and I think she's fainted. I can't find a wound, so maybe you missed her."

"No!" Kelly's face twisted with a mixture of what Longarm could only guess was outrage. "She . . ."

Kelly struggled mightily to continue speaking, but couldn't get the words out, and then he shuddered violently and was gone.

Longarm laid the man's head on the floor and watched Kelly's blood pool larger and larger on the expensive carpet. "What a tragedy you've made for us all, Lieutenant Kelly," Longarm said. "And how I wish you'd have told me exactly why you did those awful things to the chief and his wife. Right now, my bet is that you're winging your way straight down to Hell."

Longarm turned back to Abby and took her pulse, which was fast, but strong. He picked her up, laid her on the massive oak dining table, and then he went looking for some water and a towel to refresh and awaken her. No doubt poor Abby would be in shock and find it difficult to tell him exactly what had happened in those last terrible moments when Gavin Kelly had tried to murder her.

"Custis!"

He was in the hallway returning with a glass and pitcher of water he'd taken from the kitchen. Longarm hurried into the dining room and saw that Abby was sitting upright, but she was very pale and shaking badly.

"Here," he said, pouring the young woman a glass of water. "Drink this."

Abby looked up into his eyes and big tears silently rolled down her pale cheeks. "Did you . . . *kill* him?"

"No," Longarm said, "you did."

"I did?" A fresh torrent of tears cascaded down her cheeks.

"Don't you even remember?" Longarm asked.

Abby dropped her eyes and drank the water, then motioned for a second glass, which she also quickly consumed. She coughed and said, "I was in the dining room when he burst in on me. Fortunately, I was so afraid of Gavin coming that I was carrying the pistol that Mr. Stanton always kept in his bedside drawer. I didn't even know for sure if it was loaded or if I could hit anything. I was so afraid."

"Calm down," Longarm soothed. "The man is dead and

you're not even scratched. So you must have fired on instinct and you hit him at least three times. I'd say you did a remarkable job of dealing out justice."

Abby began to cry. She hugged Longarm tightly and he could feel her entire body shaking, so he said nothing for a long time.

Finally, Abby looked up at him and whispered, "It's over, Custis. The nightmare is over and I don't have to be afraid anymore. Do I?"

"No," Longarm said, thinking it unwise to suggest that the dead lieutenant might have had some accomplices. "You'll be fine now."

But Abby was thinking clearly now. "I will be if Gavin was in this by himself. But what if he had friends and they . . ."

"I'm sure he didn't," Longarm said. "I just wish that I could have taken him alive so that we could have found out exactly why he committed such a brutal outrage on Mr. Muldoon and his poor wife."

Abby looked Longarm straight in the eyes. "Why, isn't that entirely obvious?"

"What do you mean?"

"I mean that Chief Muldoon had found out about Gavin's unsavory habits and past. I'm sure that the chief meant to try and remove his rotten apple from the police force. And that would have killed Gavin because he was so vain and ambitious. So that is why Gavin felt he had no choice but to exact revenge."

"But why rape Mrs. Muldoon?"

"To make it look like the crime had no relationship to Gavin, of course."

"Yeah," Longarm said, "I guess you're right."

"Sure I am."

Abby wiped tears from her cheeks with her sleeve. "I

need to go to the hospital and see if Mr. Stanton is still alive. If he is, I want to be with him in his last moments. It's the least I can do given his years of generosity to me. And he is such a fine old gentleman. I'm really the only one left who still loves him."

"I take it he had no children?"

"None, sadly."

Longarm nodded in agreement. "I had better get the authorities here. They'll want to take a statement from us both. If there is anything that stirs them up, it is one of their own going bad."

"I don't want to look at Gavin ever again. I won't have to look at his body, will I?" she asked, almost pleading.

"No, I don't see why that would be necessary."

"I'm going to the hospital to be with Mr. Stanton right now. I have to get out of here."

"The police will want to ask you questions right away."

"I don't care! You can tell them where to find me."

Longarm decided to let her go. The Denver police would be angry that he allowed Abby to leave the scene, but they'd get over it and they'd be angry for a lot of other reasons as well.

To hell with them. At least they'll all go to bed tonight knowing that the one who nearly killed their chief and his dear wife has been brought to a swift and final justice. And that's all that really matters.

"I'll walk with you back into town," Longarm decided, realizing that he could use some fresh air. "I need to get to the police and report this at once."

"I understand."

They left the lieutenant on the floor in his wide pool of warm blood and closed the massive double front doors on their way out.

"Such a beautiful day," she said as they walked down

the porch steps. "It's hard to imagine something this terrible could happen on such a beautiful day."

"I suppose."

Abby stopped at the street and turned to gaze at the mansion for several minutes.

"It'll be yours now, won't it," Longarm said.

She tore her eyes away from the mansion and stared at him. "I . . . I suppose it will. I hadn't even thought about that. This place just seems so big and unreal to me. I've never even owned a shack, much less a mansion. But I won't keep it. No, I won't keep it a moment longer than I have to. It is already for sale. It and everything inside."

"Don't you even want to keep some things as mementos of your time with Mr. Stanton?"

"Uh . . . yes. There are a few personal items. But the house and furniture . . . no, thank you. They are much too elegant and sterile for my liking. I'll sell them for whatever the market will bear."

"You're a very rich young lady, Abby."

She looked at him with her red-rimmed eyes. "Custis, I would like to share some of what I'll receive with you."

He shook his head emphatically. "Thanks but no thanks."

"I knew you'd say that. You know that I won't be staying in Denver. I might go visit New York City. I have relatives living there that I've never even seen."

Longarm wanted to make sure he'd heard her correctly. "Did you just say that you've never been to New York?"

"No. Have you?"

"Nope." She looked so sincere and helpless with those wet tears on her cheeks that he thought The Gypsy must have gotten her past in New York City wrong. "Never have."

"Then come with me! I'll pay for everything and we can

have more fun and excitement than we've ever had in our lives."

"Abby, I'm a frontier marshal and a big Eastern city like New York would make me feel crowded."

"Are you sure?"

"Absolutely."

"Well, then," she said, trying to force a smile. "Then I'll just have to come back after my visit and tell you all about the big city."

"I have a feeling that you'll never return to this town," Longarm said, without thinking.

"Maybe you're right." Abby reached up and kissed his lips. "Thanks for helping me."

"When it came right down to it, you're the one that did what needed doing. You're a very brave woman, Miss Abby McCall."

"Sometimes . . . sometimes, perhaps we have strengths that we aren't even aware of until they're called upon in a crisis."

"Yeah," Longarm said. "Maybe that's it."

They walked into downtown Denver hand in hand and in thoughtful silence, and parted the same way.

Longarm stood on the corner and watched Abby walking eastward on West Colfax Avenue. She was pretty enough to turn men's heads, and he wondered if they had any idea of her great courage.

It wasn't until late that night when he was back in his own apartment that he realized that Abby had been walking *away from*, not *toward*, the hospital when she'd disappeared like mist on a cold winter morning.

Chapter 10

The passing of Denver philanthropist and wealthy entre-
preneur Milton Stanton was overshadowed the next morning in the local newspaper by the account of Lieutenant
Gavin Kelly's violent shooting death. Longarm was be-
sieged all that day by newspaper reporters all desperate to
know the exact circumstances of the shooting on Maple
Street and why had it occurred in Denver's wealthiest
neighborhood.

What, everyone wanted to know, was the connection between Mr. Stanton, Lieutenant Kelly, and the mysterious
Miss Abby McCall?

Longarm was advised by his boss, U.S. Marshal Billy
Vail, to answer no questions. "It's a can of worms and it
smells of rotting offal," Billy advised with an ominous shake
of his head. "How could a young woman who had never even
fired a weapon have killed a veteran police officer?"

"I don't know what to think," Longarm admitted. "I
didn't see the actual shooting, but there can be little doubt
that Abby . . . I mean Miss McCall . . . shot the lieutenant
three times in self-defense."

Billy didn't seem to be listening. "And on top of everything," he groused, "the newspapers have caught wind of the size of the inheritance that Miss McCall is to receive now that Mr. Stanton has passed on. Why, the young woman wasn't even related to Mr. Stanton! And she wasn't employed by him for that long. So everyone is sure that there is some skullduggery involved."

"Involved in what?" Longarm asked. "Mr. Stanton's death yesterday at the hospital?"

"Of course not," Billy said. "The gentleman was very old and had been in failing health for years. But this thing between Miss McCall and the dead lieutenant has the entire city buzzing. Was there a lovers' triangle?"

Longarm shrugged. "Miss McCall admitted to me that she did have an affair with the lieutenant. That's when she learned of his dark past and became suspicious that he was the one responsible for the attack on the Muldoons."

"And how about you and Miss McCall?" Billy asked, leaning forward with a scowl on his round face. "Did you also bed the woman?"

"Yes," Longarm admitted, knowing that he could not conceal the fact. "We did have a one-night stand. She came to my apartment in fear of her life. Abby knew she was going to inherit a fortune and Lieutenant Kelly wanted all of it . . . or he said he'd kill her."

Billy leaned back in his office chair and shook his head. "I just don't know," he said. "The whole thing smells like rot."

"You already said that."

"But it's true!" Billy exclaimed. "And now Miss McCall has already put the Stanton Mansion up for sale. My Gawd, she didn't even have the decency to wait until the blood was dry on the old man's Persian carpet! And do you know what else I've heard?"

"No, but I have a strong feeling that you're about to tell me."

"Miss McCall is the *executor* of the Stanton estate, and she has actually ordered the mortuary to skip a memorial service and bury the old gentleman immediately."

"No memorial service?" Longarm asked with surprise.

"None, and that's *criminal* given how many friends and admirers Mr. Stanton had in this city. Why, he was one of our most beloved philanthropists! Everyone who is anyone is outraged by this shocking news. I've been deluged by angry society people over this, and I can only imagine that the Denver Police Department, the mayor, and all the city councilmen are catching hell. People want answers and they're extremely unhappy about the way Miss McCall is going about this whole sad affair."

"I suppose I could talk to her," Longarm suggested.

"No!" Billy shouted. "I don't want your name associated in any way with that woman."

Billy jumped up from his desk chair and began to pace back and forth in his office. "Have you admitted to the newspapers that you slept with Miss McCall the night before she gunned down Lieutenant Kelly?"

"I've said nothing. And I don't think 'gunned down' is what happened. She killed the lieutenant in self-defense."

"I wonder," Billy said absently. "Tell me, Custis, did anyone see the woman coming or going from your apartment?"

"I have no idea," Longarm admitted.

Billy stopped and shook his head in disgust. "At least we have the good news that Chief Muldoon and his wife are going to recover. For that much we can be thankful."

"That's right," Longarm said.

"I'm about to leave for the hospital to pay a call of respect to Chief Muldoon. I'd like you to come along."

"I'd be honored," Longarm said, meaning it. "The chief and his wife are very close to me."

"I know that. That's why you're invited."

Billy looked up at the big clock on his wall. "Let's go now. It's my understanding that Mrs. Muldoon has already been discharged from the hospital and that her husband is expected to leave this afternoon."

Longarm started for the door, but Billy's words stopped him in his tracks. "Miss McCall did work for the Muldoons, did she not?"

Longarm turned. "Yes. What about it?"

"Well," Billy said, "then it obviously stands to reason that the chief will want to ask you some questions about her and the lieutenant. In fact, I'm sure that he will."

"I won't lie to him."

"Of course you won't," Billy said. "But Chief Muldoon and his wife have been through a very bad time, and the last thing we want is for him to get upset by something you tell him concerning Miss McCall and Lieutenant Kelly. Do you get my drift?"

"Loud and clear."

"Good," Billy said. "So when the chief asks you about the shooting death of Lieutenant Kelly, try to cover it lightly."

"And how do you cover the fact that his corrupt lieutenant was shot three times and died in my arms?" Longarm asked.

"I don't know, but think of something. And just try not to upset Chief Muldoon. He nearly died."

"He'll want to know why Lieutenant Kelly committed criminal acts against him and his wife. And he'll want to know if Kelly acted alone or had the help of someone else."

"You can't answer those questions, can you?"

"I can tell him what Abby told me."

"And do you believe what she told you?"

"I did last night."

"And what about today?" Billy asked.

Longarm remembered the look of outrage on Lieutenant Kelly's face just before he died. He added that to the fact that Abby had lied about heading directly to the hospital to be by the bedside of Mr. Stanton. And finally, he recalled The Gypsy's warning about Abby and that she had lived in New York City even though Abby had denied the fact.

"Well?" Billy asked with impatience. "Do you still believe that Miss McCall is innocent of any wrongdoing?"

"No," Longarm heard himself say. "But then again, I have no proof that she is guilty, either."

"Well, dammit, maybe you need to find out some answers and get to the bottom of this entire sordid affair."

"Yes, sir."

"But for now, try not to upset Chief Muldoon. We'd never forgive ourselves if you said something that sent him into a relapse."

"Right," Longarm said in agreement.

"Then let's go," Billy said as both men grabbed their hats and headed for the hospital.

Chapter 11

"But I thought the chief was supposed to be discharged this afternoon," Billy Vail said to the hospital nurse.

"He was, but I'm afraid that Mr. Muldoon suffered a sudden and very unexpected relapse last night."

"How serious?" Longarm asked.

"Quite serious, I'm afraid." The corners of her mouth drew down sharply. "We don't know if Mr. Muldoon will recover or not. He is being watched very closely, but we are very, very concerned."

Longarm and Billy exchanged worried glances. Longarm said, "Nurse, could you tell me the name of the doctor in charge of Chief Muldoon's care?"

She looked away for a moment, then seemed to make a decision. "That would be Dr. Wilfred Wood."

"We'd like to speak to him," Billy said. "Right now."

"I'm afraid that is not possible," the nurse said as if the matter were closed. "Dr. Wood was up all night with Mr. Muldoon, and he is both physically and mentally exhausted from his labors to keep his patient alive. Near collapse from lack of rest and mental stress, he was sent home to get some sleep."

"Nurse, I need his address," Billy said without hesitation.

The nurse, an older woman with a stern bearing, emphatically shook her head. "I'm afraid that is not possible . . . nor is it advisable. However, Dr. Wood will be back on shift tonight at eight o'clock. He might have a moment to speak to you at that time."

The nurse started to leave, but Longarm grabbed her by the arm. Not hard, but firmly, and he said, "Nurse, I know you think you are doing the right thing, but there may be murder involved. We have to find out what we can from Dr. Wood and his answers just won't wait until this evening. So I want to know if the doctor is at home with his family."

"Of course he's at his residence. But Dr. Wood is a bachelor." The nurse was big and she was strong pulling away from Longarm's grip. "Marshal, exactly *whose* murder are you talking about?"

Longarm and Billy exchanged glances, and then Billy sidestepped the question with a question of his own. "Nurse, who is looking after Chief Muldoon *right now*?"

"That would be Dr. Charles Baylor."

"We need to see him immediately."

The nurse was upset, and Longarm could see that she wanted to tell both him and Billy to go to hell, but then Billy pulled out his badge and said, "This is *urgent* federal business, Nurse. Now go find Dr. Baylor at once!"

The nurse snorted with anger and disappeared. Longarm watched her march down the hallway and commented, "That woman should have been a sergeant in the Confederate Army."

"Or the Union Army," Billy said. "She sure has gotten up on a high horse. Acts like she runs this whole damned hospital."

"Maybe she does."

A few minutes later, a small, beleaguered-looking doctor with a bald head and gray mustache rushed down the hall looking very unhappy. Longarm judged the man to be in his early sixties, and he appeared overworked and distracted by the condition of his prominent patient who was failing.

"I'm Dr. Baylor," he snapped, ignoring Billy's outstretched hand. "What is so important that I had to be called away from my patients?"

"Is there a room where we can talk in private?" Billy asked, ignoring the man's rudeness. "What I have to tell you is quite sensitive."

"And what I'm dealing with is life and death!" Dr. Baylor shouted, demonstrating that he was near the breaking point.

"It will only take a moment. We can talk here," Billy said smoothly, "or you can come down to the Federal Building and we'll talk there in my office. So which is it to be, Dr. Baylor?"

"All right. All right!" the small man growled. "We can talk in the linen room. But I only have a few minutes. A very few minutes. Mr. Muldoon is hanging onto life by a thread, and it really galls me that you're here trying to interfere with and intimidate me."

"Only a few minutes, Doctor," Longarm said reassuringly. "If it wasn't of critical importance, believe me, we would not be interrupting you at this time."

Dr. Baylor gave him a go-to-hell look and hurried off yelling, "Our linen room is right down here. Come along!"

"Friendly fella," Billy groused.

"He's under a lot of pressure to save the chief," Longarm said. "And Muldoon's unexpected and sudden setback must have the poor man baffled and extremely upset."

When they were in the small linen room, Dr. Baylor glared and said, "Let's hear what you have to say in a very

75

few words. Because, if you men try to obstruct me any longer than that, you'd better have an arrest warrant."

Longarm looked to Billy because he was the senior man. Billy said, "Doctor, did you read about the shoot-out at Mr. Stanton's home and how a woman named Miss McCall killed a Lieutenant Kelly?"

Even more agitated, Dr. Baylor cried, "Yes, but what possible—"

"Do you know Miss McCall?"

"I've seen her here many times the last few weeks. She's been visiting both Mr. Stanton before he died as well as Chief Muldoon. But I still—"

"Be just a little more patient," Billy asked. "What we have to say is to be kept in strict confidence."

Dr. Baylor was losing control. "Don't shilly-shally around, Marshal! Spit out what you have to say and what possible connection this conversation has with my dying patient!"

Longarm was a far bigger and more imposing man than his boss, and now he felt the need to lean in toward the doctor and say, "We think that Miss McCall murdered Lieutenant Kelly as well as Mr. Milburn Stanton . . . for the money she is inheriting. And also she might be trying to murder your current patient, Chief Muldoon . . . by poisoning."

"What!"

The light was poor in the linen room, but it was good enough to show that Dr. Baylor had turned about three shades lighter. "That's . . . that's medically impossible!"

"It isn't," Longarm insisted. "Especially if she had the help of someone who knew the chemical interaction between medicines and poisons. I'm talking about a scientist . . . pharmacist . . . or a smart *doctor* with an evil and secret agenda."

Dr. Baylor blanched and staggered. "You're not suggesting that I—"

"No," Longarm said. "How old is Mr. Muldoon's primary doctor?"

"You mean Dr. Wood?"

Longarm nodded, himself now even more impatient than the doctor, who appeared close to a mental breakdown.

"He's . . . he's in his thirties," Dr. Baylor murmured. "But—"

"And a bachelor. Might he have found Miss McCall attractive?"

"She *is* attractive. I'm old, but I'm not blind! So what if Dr. Wood felt attracted to the poor young woman."

"She is anything but poor now," Billy said in a tone that was flat and hard.

"But that has nothing to do with my colleague Dr. Wood!"

"We need to make sure of that," Longarm said. "I'm told that both Mr. Stanton and Chief Muldoon had sudden bad turns in their health. Isn't that true?"

"Yes," Baylor admitted with reluctance.

"And since you work here, you probably have served both patients. Have you seen similarities in their sudden downturns?"

Dr. Baylor was now leaning against the linen closet and looking as if his skinny legs were about to buckle. "Actually," he whispered, "their symptoms and sudden health failures are . . . are quite similar. Vomiting. Sudden loss of blood pressure and pulse rate. Slight yellowing of the skin. Tremor in the extremities that remains unexplainable. Urine that has a very distinct, but unfamiliar, odor and color. Blood in their stools."

"Common symptoms of poisoning?" Longarm asked quietly.

"But also of some rare diseases. Rare diseases that they could not have contracted in Colorado and perhaps not even in the United States."

"Unless they were imported and then injected or swallowed with some contaminant," Longarm said. "Some element that a man of science might be able to obtain from a distant source."

Dr. Baylor was no longer abrasive or confident. Instead, he seemed to have aged considerably in the last few moments. He stammered, "I could run some tests. Administer medicines, antidotes that coat the stomach and would impede the absorption of any . . . any poisonous elements that might have recently been administered to Chief Muldoon."

"Do that," Billy said. "Do it now, but first tell us where we can find Dr. Wood."

Dr. Baylor readily gave them the man's address, which was in one of Denver's higher-class neighborhoods. The shaken physician ended up stammering, "I just can't believe that Dr. Wood might have accidentally poisoned Chief Muldoon or Mr. Stanton."

"If he did it," Longarm said through gritted teeth as he slammed open the linen door, "I promise you it wasn't him alone and it sure wasn't any damned accident."

Chapter 12

Longarm and Billy were both packing pistols under their coats as they hurried across town to find and question Dr. Wood.

"I'm afraid that I have a bad feeling about this," Longarm told his boss. "Real bad."

"Do you really think that Dr. Wood and Miss McCall were partners in murdering Stanton and putting Chief Muldoon back on death's doorstep?"

"It seems likely," Longarm replied. "Think about it and you'll see it adds up. Lieutenant Kelly hated the chief, so he was the one that broke into the man's house and nearly beat him to death and then raped Mrs. Muldoon. But it was all planned that way to throw off the authorities. A careful plot to hide the true motives behind some crazy-appearing act of vengeance."

"I can see that," Billy said, puffing as he tried to match Longarm's tremendous stride. "And then Miss McCall also had this Dr. Wood totally entranced and in her power, and she probably told the doctor that she would make him a wealthy man after she inherited the Stanton fortune."

"No doubt," Longarm said, "it's the same promise I'm

sure she made to Lieutenant Kelly. Only neither dupe knew about the other."

"If what you're saying is true, then this Miss McCall has the heart of a monster and the wiles of a Jezebel."

"I don't know about the monster part," Longarm quietly admitted, "but I can testify to the woman's power to seduce a man and at least temporarily rob him of reason."

"She did that to you, didn't she." It wasn't a question.

Longarm didn't glance sideways at his boss as they hurried along the busy downtown streets on their way to interview Dr. Wood. "All I can say," Longarm replied, "is that Abby McCall has the talent and the body to make a man do pretty much whatever she wants."

"Was she also planning on trapping *you* in her deadly web?"

"I thought about that some," Longarm confessed. "And I'm not sure what she wanted from me, but given time, I'll probably come up with the answers. I do know now that that woman is a schemer and seductress. I don't quite know where I fit into her plans unless it was that she wanted me to kill the lieutenant. That would have been neater, but I didn't walk that path and she had to kill Kelly herself."

"If Wood confesses, he'll hang and so will Miss McCall. Woman or not, she'll hang," Billy panted, winded and sweating profusely as he tried to keep up with Longarm.

Longarm agreed. "I expect so and they'll both deserve to hang. Mr. Stanton couldn't have had many years left, but Lieutenant Kelly was in his prime, and then there are the Muldoons who have suffered so much."

"If the chief dies," Billy wheezed, "Miss McCall will have been the direct cause of three men dying."

"There could even be a *fourth*," Longarm said quietly.

"Who . . ." Billy Vail was badly out of shape and completely out of breath. "You don't think that Miss McCall might have already murdered Dr. Wood, do you?"

"That possibility has crossed my mind in the last few minutes," Longarm answered, wishing his boss was in better condition and this chase across Denver wasn't taking so long.

"Oh, my Gawd!"

Shocked by the possibility of a fourth murder, Billy started to run, but his short legs and fat body couldn't stand the strain and he quickly stopped, bent over, and struggled for breath. "I'm slowing you down, Custis. Go on without me. Hurry! You might be able to stop her before she murders Dr. Wood!"

Longarm needed no urging and began to sprint, causing people on the street to part before him. The address he'd been given by Dr. Baylor was up a hill and about three blocks to the west. The neighborhood was a mix of nice homes and very elegant apartments where the upper class tended to live. Dr. Wood would be young and successful, and he fit as the kind of man that Abby McCall would have sought out to be her partner in murder.

The way Longarm had it figured, if Dr. Wood was Abby's accomplice, the man deserved to die, but not by being poisoned or shot by the treacherous Abby. No, what the doctor really deserved would be a hangman's rope.

Chapter 13

Longarm had some trouble finding Dr. Wood's place of residence. But when he did, he ran directly up the stairs and hammered on the door. "Dr. Wood!"

There was no answer and the door was unlocked. Longarm entered a well-decorated home with expensive furnishings. "Dr. Wood. I'm Deputy United States Marshal Custis Long."

He might as well have stopped and caught his breath because there was no answer, and when Longarm went into the doctor's bedroom, he saw the completely naked physician lying facedown on a very large but rumpled four-poster bed.

Longarm rolled Dr. Wood over and touched the man's flushed face. The skin was still a little warm, telling him that rigor mortis hadn't set in completely. And although he was no expert in these matters, Longarm thought that the physician could not have died more than a few hours earlier.

"Damn!" Longarm muttered to himself. "He probably deserved his fate, but this means that he sure isn't going to give us any answers or testimony."

Longarm stood and looked around the room. He was

careful not to rearrange anything as he observed every detail. The bed had been slept in the night before and it had two pillows, both indented by the weight of heads. Longarm observed several long hairs that were the same color as Abby's. The apartment was tidy, but the kitchen sink was filled with dirty dishes. There was an empty bottle of French wine, the kind that an officer of the law could not afford to buy, and it was obvious that the doctor had entertained the previous evening.

"And I'd bet my last dollar that it was Abby that he wined and dined, then bedded. I wonder if he got her to . . . well, never mind. But he *is* sort of smiling."

Actually, the doctor wore a death grin with his lips pulled far back from his teeth more in a grimace of intense pain than of pleasure. Longarm shook his head and began to carefully search the house for any kind of evidence that might prove useful.

"Custis!"

It was an exhausted Billy standing in the doorway bent over and gasping for air. His round face was streaked with perspiration and he looked like his heart was about to burst from overexertion.

"Dr. Wood is lying on his bed," Longarm said. "His body hasn't gone cold yet so I'd guess he died sometime this morning."

"Any wounds or sign of a fight?"

"No," Longarm said. "I wouldn't swear to it, but it appears he was poisoned."

Billy took several deep breaths and went into the bedroom. Longarm heard his boss take in a sharp breath, and then he started searching again for any evidence that would implicate Abby McCall as the murderess.

Billy came out of the bedroom with a look of shock and amazement on his sweaty face. "The doctor is smiling."

84

"Yeah," Longarm said cryptically. "Abby is that good in bed."

"You're lucky it isn't you lying in there instead of the doctor," Billy said, faintly accusing. "The way you bed strange women, I'm surprised that you haven't been murdered by a spurned woman or shot by an enraged husband years ago."

Longarm turned and looked across the room at his boss. "I can't speak for the husbands, but I always leave my women satisfied and happy."

"Yeah," Billy replied, "I bet that was what that doctor in there thought, too."

Longarm was opening kitchen cabinets and searching for something, although he was not sure what. "Well, look at this!"

Billy hurried over. "What is it?"

Longarm reached up into a top cabinet shelf and produced something white and powdery in a small glass jar. "It could just be baking soda or corn flour," Longarm said, unscrewing the jar's cap and sniffing it. "Or it could be the chemical that poisoned Dr. Wood and the others."

"Put your tongue to it and give it a taste."

"The hell with that," Longarm shot back, sniffing the contents. "We'll have a chemist analyze it. It's odorless and probably tasteless."

"Then it would be a perfect poison," Billy said.

"Yes," Longarm agreed, "it would be. Maybe you should go find the doctor's desk."

"How do you know he even has one?"

"Just a hunch. And when you find it, see if you can find out where Dr. Wood does his banking. Also, if he wrote anything that we might use to pin these murders on Abby McCall."

But Billy hesitated. "I think we should back out of here

and let the Denver Police Department do the investigating. They'd be pretty upset if they knew we were intruding on their case."

"Piss on 'em," Longarm said without passion. "If we let them come in here, then they might miss something. Or mess up some important evidence. I'm going to stay right here for a little while until I'm satisfied that I've done my best to uncover any clues or links to Abby."

Their eyes locked and then Billy said, "All right. We'll close the front door and look around a while longer. But we won't move or mess up anything so that they can have the same chance that we are getting. Fair enough?"

"Fair enough," Longarm agreed.

"That means you have to put that jar back on the top shelf."

"Fine," Longarm said, "but not before I take some of the powder so that our own chemist has a chance to analyze it."

"You don't seem to have much faith in the Denver Police Department."

"It isn't that," Longarm explained, "as much as it is having more faith in myself."

"Cocky bastard."

Longarm ignored the comment and continued to search. Going back in the bedroom, he found a smear of lipstick on the pillow. It was the same shade that Abby wore the night she'd come calling at his apartment. He knew that because there was still lipstick on his own pillow. He also found a few drops of blood on the bathroom floor.

Had Dr. Wood merely cut himself shaving, or perhaps accidentally pricked his finger?

Longarm went back and examined the corpse more closely.

"What are you doing?" Billy asked.

"Maybe I missed something important on the body." Longarm looked up at his boss. "Did you find his desk?"

"Yes."

"Any papers or bank statements?"

"I haven't gotten that far yet," Billy replied.

"Time is wasting."

"Who's in charge here, anyway?" Billy demanded, looking insulted.

"You are," Longarm told him.

"Well, it doesn't sound that way."

Longarm rolled Dr. Wood back over onto his stomach. "Sorry, Boss. It's just that maybe you've been pushing a pencil and riding a desk too many years while I've been out in the field looking at murder victims. Speaking of which, look closer here at the doctor's buttock."

"Do I have to?"

"It's important."

Billy bent over beside Longarm, who said, "Do you see the dried blood?"

"It looks like a mole."

"It isn't," Longarm said, taking out a small penknife from his pocket and scraping away a little blood. "See?"

"Yeah." Billy appeared disgusted. "It isn't everyday that I have to inspect a dead man's ass."

"He's been stuck," Longarm said, ignoring the comment. "Most likely by a needle."

"You mean like the ones attached to a syringe?"

"Yeah," Longarm said, "a syringe filled with something that he didn't want injected into his body. Maybe the white, odorless powder in a solution."

Billy stood up. "Are you suggesting that Miss McCall injected her poison into Dr. Wood rather than mixing it into a drink or his food?"

"I don't know," Longarm confessed. "It's possible Abby could have done both. Maybe the doctor, knowing about the poison, was too wary to have swallowed anything Abby gave him. And so perhaps she got him drunk, screwed his brains out, and then when he was asleep and lying naked on his belly, she injected him with a big dose of the poison. Enough to kill him almost instantly so that the man didn't struggle."

"You're making a lot of assumptions," Billy said, looking skeptical.

"Sure I am," Longarm replied, "but do you have any better explanations? Dr. Wood must have been the one that helped her kill Mr. Stanton and almost kill Chief Muldoon in the hospital. So he would have been too careful to have trusted Abby given the amount of money involved in the inheritance. But if they'd made love and he was half drunk and asleep, she could easily have injected him with a lethal dose."

"I guess it really does make a lot of sense."

Longarm stood up and said, "Where's the doctor's desk?"

"Two doors down. Nice little office and a desk as big as my own and a leather desk chair that must have set him back at least a hundred dollars."

"Did Dr. Wood have a lot of scientific and medical books?"

"Dozens," Billy confirmed.

"And I'll bet that some of them are about poisons," Longarm said, heading out of the room. "Not that I'll be able to understand the chemistry."

"We have people that can do that."

"Then let's do our best to find out what elements might have been used in these murders," Longarm said. "And if the doctor left any evidence on paper as to his involvement with Abby."

"I'd say that was highly unlikely."

"Maybe not as unlikely as you'd think," Longarm said. "Have you ever heard of someone leaving a death note as insurance in case they were double-crossed by a murderer?"

"Can't say as I have."

"Me neither," Longarm told his boss, "but it seems reasonable that someone as intelligent and educated as Dr. Wood just might have written or left some kind of evidence just in case he was betrayed and murdered by Abby."

Billy nodded with sudden excitement. "Custis, you're even better at this kind of thing than I thought you were."

"I'm no fool," Longarm said.

"Except when it comes to women. Remember, you slept with Abby McCall."

"Sure I did and I wouldn't trade the experience for anything."

"Yeah, well, what if she'd have injected you in the ass with a needle?"

"I'd have come off the bed jumpin' and fightin'," Longarm told Billy. "And I'd have gone for her throat and snapped her neck a second before my heart stopped beating."

Billy stared at Longarm. Finally, he said, "Yeah, I believe you would have."

"Damn right. Now let's get into that office and get to work. We'll give ourselves an hour. If we don't find anything by then, my belief is that it doesn't exist."

Billy looked back over his shoulder into the bedroom. "What a waste. Dr. Wood was young, handsome, and obviously had the world by the tail. Why would he ever have gotten involved with a whore and murderess like Abby McCall?"

"It's my experience that women are usually more clever and devious than men," Longarm said after giving the question a moment of careful thought. "And don't forget . . . Abby has been around a while but she is pretty enough to make a man lose his senses and do stupid things."

"Maybe."

"Maybe hell," Longarm said. "And when you add in the fortune that Abby is inheriting . . . well, it's an almost irresistible and highly fatal combination."

"So how'd you escape her deadly web?" Billy asked.

Longarm gave him a cold smile. "Abby hadn't gotten around to bribing me with any inheritance money yet."

"What if she had?"

"Who knows? It would have been nice to have been rich for the first time in my life instead of just another underpaid and unappreciated lawman."

Billy's eyes widened and then he snorted. "Deputy Long, you are a real piece of work."

"Thank you, Boss."

Chapter 14

Longarm and Billy were both greatly relieved when they received the news that Chief Muldoon had survived his latest hospital crisis. However, just a few moments earlier, the Denver Police Department's top officials and two of their detectives had arrived at the federal office building upset and with plenty of questions concerning the death of Dr. Wood, Lieutenant Kelly, and Milburn Stanton.

"It's a damned shame that you federal people aren't being open with our department," Captain May complained as he and his colleagues stood crowded around Billy Vail's desk with fire in their eyes.

"Now take it easy, Captain," Billy said, trying to soothe the captain and his men, "because we were planning on sharing all our latest information with your department."

"When!" Captain May angrily demanded.

Longarm had never seen his boss shouted at before, and he was totally surprised when Billy came to his feet and shouted back, "Tomorrow! And if you raise your voice at me again, Captain, I'll have you and your people escorted straight out of this federal building and I'll be damned if I'll voluntarily cooperate with you."

91

The captain was a big man and not used to someone coming back at him with his own anger. Billy's response had surprised him and he drew a deep breath, then said, "All right. All right, Marshal Vail. We *are* hot under the collar, but you ought to understand why. Chief Muldoon and his wife were almost murdered, and Lieutenant Kelly was shot to death under circumstances that do not reflect favorably on our department. So everything is pretty fouled up right now and the press is climbing up and down my back wanting answers."

"We believe that your lieutenant was very much involved in a murder conspiracy," Longarm said, looking over his boss's head at the police captain.

"Bullshit!" May roared. "Can you prove it?"

"Not yet," Longarm said, keeping his own temper under tight control. "But had we been able to get to Dr. Wood before he died, we think we'd have been able to get a confession out of the man."

Captain May put his hands on his hips and glared. "So you have no proof whatsoever."

"That's right," Billy said.

"Did you search Dr. Wood's apartment?"

"We looked it over."

"And?"

Billy stood up from his desk. "Captain, I was about to tell you that we found a powder that we think could be the poison that killed Dr. Wood and Mr. Stanton and almost killed your Chief Muldoon."

"Where the hell is that powder now!" May shouted, looking aghast and outraged. "Marshal Vail, do you mean to tell me that you *removed* the poison without even asking us?"

Longarm shook his head. "Captain, are you saying that

your investigators didn't even find the poison in Dr. Wood's kitchen cabinet?"

May was thrown completely off guard. He whirled around to look at his two best detectives. "Do you know what Long is talking about?"

"No," they both said in unison.

Longarm knew that he had them in an embarrassing fix, but he also understood that this was not the time or the place to turn the screw and make them look even more incompetent, so he said, "There is a jar in an upper kitchen cabinet that contains a mysterious white powder. It's odorless and probably tasteless . . . although I wouldn't recommend you tasting it. It's very probably the poison used in the murders."

"How could you possibly jump to that conclusion?" one of the detectives said in a sarcastic voice directed at Longarm.

"Easy," Longarm answered. "We noticed that Dr. Wood had a spot of blood on his left buttock."

"Maybe he sat on a pin," the detective said, grinning as if he had made a good joke.

"Maybe," Longarm said, ignoring the man's ignorance and biting sarcasm. "But a better guess would be that Dr. Wood was injected . . . probably with a solution made from that white powder."

The Denver Police Department people all exchanged glances. Then Captain May barked, "Lewis, you and Don apparently missed that jar. Go over to the doctor's place, get it and have it analyzed by our chemistry department, and get me the results at once!"

The two detectives weren't smirking at Longarm anymore. They shot out of Billy's office as if their own asses had been stabbed. When they were gone, Captain May took a deep breath. "Marshal Vail, the feds and our department have always been quick to cooperate fully with each other. I think we should be doing that right now."

"I fully agree that we should cooperate, but it's not true that we've done it in the past," Billy said without anger. "You people have always been secretive and uncooperative with those of us who wear a federal officer's badge. However, since this case does involve your chief, we're forgetting the past and trying our damnedest to be of service to your fine department."

Captain May was mollified by the compliment. "So who do you think is behind all this and why?"

Billy turned to Longarm and said, "Custis, why don't you try to explain since you know who we think is the prime suspect."

Longarm would have preferred to have remained silent, but now there was no choice. In as few words as necessary, he explained why the most likely murder suspect was Miss Abby McCall. He ended up his brief summation by saying, "We believe Miss McCall had the help of first your Lieutenant Kelly. Then, when she shot him to death claiming self-defense, she turned on her next coconspirator, Dr. Wood, and injected him with poison. She did all of this because the woman is going to inherit a fortune from the Stanton estate."

"I find it difficult to believe that she could have corrupted both Lieutenant Kelly and Dr. Wood, two men of high intelligence and accomplishment."

"Well," Longarm said, "I'm afraid that she did corrupt them. And I don't find it so hard to believe since she has all that inheritance money coming her way from the Stanton estate and would have used it to bribe both men. And have you ever seen Miss McCall?"

"No," Captain May confessed. "And why are you asking?"

"If you had seen the woman, then you'd understand how she could have done it because Miss McCall is not only extremely attractive, but she is very clever and seductive."

"And you have firsthand knowledge of that, I suppose?" Captain May bluntly asked.

When Longarm didn't reply, the captain added, "Custis, I don't mean to insult you, but your reputation as a lady's man is common knowledge in this town . . . has been for years."

"I'm not a bit insulted," Longarm answered. "And as for Miss McCall, I can tell you that we only recently met when she came to my apartment one night frightened and fearful for her life. She said that Lieutenant Kelly was demanding to get all of her future inheritance . . . or he would kill her."

Captain May snorted with disbelief. "And you believed the woman?"

"I admit that I did at first."

"And what made you change your mind?"

"Many things," Longarm said, not willing to mention The Gypsy's warnings about Abby. "It just all added up that Miss McCall had the most to gain by Mr. Stanton's death. Chief Muldoon and his wife were all a diversion . . . a pretty effective one, I might add."

"Where can we find Miss McCall?"

"I have no idea," Longarm admitted. "But since she does stand to inherit the Stanton Mansion, I would think that she would have to hang around until the legal matter of the estate is satisfied."

"Not so," Billy said. "The woman will probably have an attorney handle everything including the legal transfer and sale of the mansion and all of the old gentleman's assets. What I'm saying is that Abby McCall could be in Europe and still have everything handled and arranged by an attorney right here in Denver."

"Well, we'll just have to put an end to that!" Captain May exclaimed. "Who is her attorney?"

"I have no idea," Billy replied. "Custis?"

"None."

May looked confused. "Then how will we . . ."

"Footwork," Longarm explained. "You'll have to knock on every attorney's door and try to find out if Abby retained them to handle the inheritance. But I will tell you this . . . they won't talk."

"They had damned well better talk."

"They won't," Longarm said with certainty. "Abby will have hired an attorney to handle the affair in the strictest confidence. When the estate is settled, it may be on public record, but until then, Captain May, you're most likely to be completely stonewalled."

The Denver Police Department official suddenly appeared as if he were about to have a screaming fit. Both Billy and Longarm watched as the man struggled for self-control by pacing back and forth on Billy's carpet. Finally, May turned on them and said, "Let me summarize what we have here, gentlemen. We have no evidence. No witnesses. No any damned thing that we can use to arrest Miss McCall . . . even if we do find her, and I promise you that we will."

"That's about the size of it," Billy agreed, not looking the least bit upset. "And even if your chemistry department identifies the powder as the poison that killed Dr. Wood and almost caused Chief Muldoon to have a fatal relapse at the hospital, we still can't prove that the deadly and seductive Miss McCall is the guilty party."

"Because?" May asked with obvious exasperation.

"Because there are no living witnesses except Chief Muldoon. And when you ask him if he was poisoned, he won't know because he has been getting a lot of medicines during his hospital stay, any one of which could have been a poison given by an unsuspecting doctor or nurse."

"Damnation!" Captain May shouted. "And to top it all off, this . . . this viper woman is going to become rich?"

"Yep," Longarm said. "Very, very rich."

"But there must be some way we can get her to . . ."

"To what?" Longarm asked, eyes narrowing at the frustrated captain. "To confess? Why would she do that? She's much too clever."

"So this murdering whore goes scot-free?"

Longarm shook his head with conviction. "She had Lieutenant Kelly rape Mrs. Muldoon and beat the chief nearly to death. She shot Kelly down, and even though he was in cahoots with her, he didn't deserve to die like that. And finally, she made love to Dr. Wood, then jammed poison into his poor, trusting ass. Because of all those criminal acts, she can't walk away from this free and wealthy. Abby McCall *has* to pay."

May said, "I agree! We all agree. But you just said there are no living witnesses and no evidence."

"Not so far as we know," Longarm told the man. "But I'm not about to give up and neither should you or your detectives . . . even though they couldn't even find that jar of what is probably the poison."

Suddenly, Captain May looked defeated and physically ill. "I need to go back to my office and think about all this for a while. I don't see any light at the end of this dark and bloody tunnel. Not a crack of it."

"See if your chemistry department confirms that the white powder is some kind of unusual poison, Captain.

Then see if you can track down the source of that poison and maybe . . . just maybe it will lead to Miss McCall."

"Sure," the captain said, not looking a bit optimistic. "And there might be written evidence at Wood's residence. An incriminating note. Something solid."

"That's right," Longarm said, feeling sorry for the man. "You've hardly begun to investigate."

"Okay then," Captain May said, shooting a hard look at his remaining men. "Let's go."

"We'll be in touch if we come up with anything," Billy called as the Denver police officers scrambled out of his office.

Longarm closed the door and turned to Billy. "I'd say that went as well as could be expected."

"No, it didn't. We didn't tell him everything."

"You could have told him a few more details," Longarm agreed, "but he got the meat of it."

"How are you going to find Miss McCall and get her to confess to everything?"

Longarm shrugged. "I have no idea, Boss."

"You'll think of something," Billy told him. "Because I'm pretty sure that you're the only one that can bring her to justice."

"I'll give it all my best," Longarm promised.

"Custis?"

"Yeah?"

"Before you leave, I want to tell you that I just got word from our chemist that you were right about the powder . . . it is a very unusual and lethal poison."

"What's it called?"

"I forgot. Some long chemical name that neither of us ever heard of."

"Where can it be bought?"

"In China. It is extracted from a Chinese root. It's rare

98

and quite expensive. It has been used by Chinese royalty to poison other unsuspecting Chinese royalty as long as the written word has existed."

"Hmm," Longarm mused. "Then I guess I had better go into our Chinatown and start asking questions about that poison and about Dr. Wood."

"Even though the Chinese are among the most secretive people I've ever come across, why not?" Billy said, looking almost as defeated as had Captain May. "Because, frankly, I don't know what else you can do until Miss McCall reappears . . . if she ever does."

"She won't," Longarm predicted. "At least not in Denver she won't."

"Do you have any idea where to pick up her trail?"

"Maybe New York City."

Billy started. "Why . . ."

"Never mind," Longarm said. "It's a long story and a very thin thread. I'd only use it as a last resort."

"Good," Billy said, "because we can't afford to send you."

"Somehow I knew that you would say that."

"Custis?" Billy called as Longarm was leaving.

"Yeah?"

"If you do find the woman, just kill her."

Longarm frowned. "Boss, are you serious?"

"I don't know," Billy said, running his fingers through his thinning hair. "But if I were you, that's what I'd do before she killed me."

"Aw," Longarm said, "she wouldn't try do that. At least not until the morning after."

"Get out of here," Billy said with mock gruffness. "Just bring her to justice."

"I'll do my best," Longarm said as he was leaving.

Chapter 15

Longarm left the office and began to walk the streets as he considered what his first move should be to try to locate Abby McCall. He realized that it was very possible that Abby had gone underground right here in Denver while she sorted out some things relating to her inheritance. For instance, she might want to return to the Stanton Mansion if she knew that there was a secret safe or hiding place containing jewelry and cash.

Cash.

Abby would need cash if she were to stay in hiding or leave town. She'd be too smart just to board the train, and Longarm was quite sure that Captain May would have that escape route well covered by his men as they combed the town for Abby.

So the woman would have to travel by private conveyance. And that would be difficult and expensive. She'd need all the money she could lay her hands on both for the escape and to pay an attorney to keep his silence and to handle the vast and valuable Stanton estate.

Where would Abby go after she had the cash and had an attorney?

Longarm really didn't have a clue. It was a hell of a lot harder trying to guess what a woman would do instead of a man.

So with all these questions rolling around in Longarm's mind, he walked the streets of Denver until well after dark completely oblivious of his surroundings and the people who passed him by while he was deep in thought.

"Yoo-hoo! Anyone at home?"

Longarm felt a light tap on his shoulder and turned to see The Gypsy standing behind him with a smile on her lovely face. "I've been trying to catch up to you for the last block, but you were so deep in thought and walking so fast I'd about given up. Fortunately, you finally had to stop for that freight wagon."

"Hi," he said, pulling himself back to the present. "It's good to see you again."

"That's the answer I was hoping to hear," she said, standing up on her toes and giving him a kiss on the lips. Then she slipped her arm through his and said, "Custis, darling, you look lost and sad. I'm going to take you home and cheer you up with good drink, song, and then love-making. How does that sound?"

"As nice as that all sounds, I'm not sure that I can afford to take the time right now," he said, knowing it was the wrong thing to say, but it was honest. "I've got a lot of troubles on my mind."

"And that would be concerning your Miss Abby McCall."

"She isn't *mine*. Never was or will be," he blurted out. "Cripes, I'm lucky I wasn't poisoned or shot along with the other fools who sampled her delights."

"Yes," The Gypsy said. "You're pretty lucky all right. And don't forget that I was the one that warned you . . . and perhaps saved your life."

"I haven't forgotten. Did you hear about the death of Dr. Wilbur Wood? He only lived about three blocks from here."

"Oh, I heard about it all right," the woman replied. "And I was pretty sure that Miss McCall had something to do with the young doctor's death."

"How did you guess?"

"I have eyes everywhere telling me what goes on in this town," The Gypsy said with a smile. "Plus, I actually saw that poor fool of a doctor and Miss McCall walking together late one evening. The conversation they were having was not a pleasant one, I can well assure you."

"They were fighting?"

"Arguing passionately," The Gypsy answered. "I hurried after them, but they turned into the doctor's apartment before I could get close enough to overhear their heated conversation. That disappointed me greatly."

Longarm had to smile. "Do you often walk alone at night eavesdropping?"

"Of course not!" she said, trying to look insulted but failing. "However, I do like to take my exercise at night. As you well know, Big Boy."

Longarm blushed at her meaning. "Yes, I *do* know."

"So, come home with me and we can have a nice time and share information about poor Dr. Wood and Miss Mc-Call . . . even though that is certainly not her real name."

Longarm nodded because he knew that The Gypsy might be able to help him answer some of the dark questions that were plaguing him, and also because he knew that he would enjoy her company and her bed.

It was about eleven o'clock at night and Longarm was riding The Gypsy for all he was worth. She had her legs wrapped around his waist and he was jamming his big rod in and out as deep and as fast as he could.

"Come on, darling! Give it *all* to me! Don't hold back an inch."

"I'm not," he told her, panting and sweating as he worked to bring her to a climax.

"Roll over and let me be on top!"

"You were on top a little while ago."

"I know."

Longarm wouldn't let the woman back on top, and after another five minutes of hard pounding, he felt The Gypsy's body start to spasm wildly a moment before she cried out with pleasure as they both found shuddering ecstasy.

"Oh, my heavens," The Gypsy gasped, clutching him tightly. "That one took a lot longer than the last, but it was worth the wait!"

Longarm rolled off her with his chest heaving in and out. "Three times in three hours. You've about wrung me out."

She giggled and turned to kiss his cheek, then rub his chest until it ceased its rapid rise and fall. "Custis, you are the best," she said. "And I like you."

He turned to look into her eyes. "I like you, too. How come you never took a husband and had children?"

"Why? Are you thinking along those lines? We'd have some beautiful girls and tall, handsome sons, you and me."

"I guess we would at that. But it's not the path in life that either of us has chosen."

"And right now," she said, "you're feeling as if you are in a box with no way out to find Abby McCall."

"Sorta," he admitted. "She's responsible for a lot of death and she's going to be rich. We don't have a shred of evidence against her even if she showed up in my office tomorrow. I kind of feel like she's outsmarted all of us and she must be laughing all the way to the bank."

The Gypsy sat up and smiled a crooked smile. "You know, in my experience, when it seems that nothing works and most everything is going wrong, I've found that you just need to work a little harder. Give it another try or even a fresh outlook."

"I know that Abby poisoned Mr. Stanton, but he's already been buried. She poisoned Dr. Wood and he's in the morgue. And finally, she almost managed to poison Chief Muldoon, but he's so tough he somehow pulled through. And we've even found the poison . . . it's rare and comes from China. But we can't connect the woman to any of this and it's driving me crazy."

"I know people in Chinatown."

"You do?"

"Of course. Important people."

Longarm was suddenly hopeful. "Do you think that you could find out—"

"Of course," she said, interrupting. "Why don't we get dressed and go to Chinatown."

"Tonight?"

"Yes," The Gypsy said. "The man who might be able to help us cannot be visited in the daytime."

"And you think he would know about this poison?"

The Gypsy nodded. "I would almost bet on it. And he would know of anyone who has bought some of it who was not Chinese. This old man knows everything that goes on in Chinatown. Just like I try to know everything about Denver . . . and men who strongly attract me. Men like *you*."

Longarm jumped out of bed. "If you can help me on this I would be very grateful."

"We'll do what we can," The Gypsy promised. "I'm not

only doing this for you, Custis. I'm doing it for Mr. and Mrs. Muldoon, who are my friends."

Longarm nodded with understanding and then he began to get dressed. If this woman could help him tie Abby to the rare poison, that would be the first real evidence that he would have against her.

Chapter 16

Longarm was aware that the Chinese in America had always been the butt of bad jokes and ridicule. Most had come across the Pacific with the dream of earning a little wealth, then returning to China and living an easier life. When gold had first been discovered at Sutter's Mill in 1848, the Chinese had poured across the ocean to work the cold, swift Sierra streams, but they were allowed to work only the streams and rivers that had already been panned out by the whites. Such claims provided barely a subsistence living, but the Chinese were hardworking and thrifty enough to live on just a little hard-won pay dirt. They didn't mind taking claims that the whites labeled as "not having a Chinaman's chance" of yielding any more gold.

Almost two decades later, when even the Chinese could not find enough flakes of the yellow metal to scratch out a living, they were asked to help build the Central Pacific Railroad in the great race to connect rails from Omaha to Sacramento. The Chinese were imported by the thousands to lay track up the western slope of the mighty Sierra Nevada Mountains. They worked without complaint or whiskey, needing only a little food and opium, which they smoked in their ceremonial joss houses.

The great railroad barons admitted that, without the sober and hardworking Chinese, the Central Pacific would never have been able to scale the Sierra Nevada Mountains and then forge on across the deserts of Nevada to connect with the Union Pacific Railroad at Promontory Point, Utah. And on that historic day in 1869, when the golden spike was driven connecting the two great railroads, not a photograph, a thank-you, or even a hint of recognition was given to the thousands of Chinese workmen who had sacrificed and died laying the rails eastward.

When all the Western railroads had been built and the gold strikes were pretty much over, many Chinese finally returned to their homeland, leaving their brethren behind in mostly unmarked graves. But some had gotten used to the strange ways of America and chose to remain. They did not learn English nor did they accept Christianity, instead choosing to huddle and even prosper in small communities located in the worst neighborhoods of the Western cities like San Francisco, Reno, Seattle, and Denver. After the Civil War, they asked only to be allowed to live apart and without persecution by the whites. And so they worked industriously and kept their ways intact, and kept their seemingly strange practices to themselves.

But The Gypsy knew the Chinese because she had studied their ways and found many of them highly intelligent and to her liking. She had cultivated a few close Chinese friends, and sometimes used their medicines to her advantage, and she loved their spicy food and smooth rice wine. Occasionally, The Gypsy also smoked their opium pipes, knowing that she was among friends during her time spent floating among the ethereal vapors of nirvana.

* * *

"This is the place," The Gypsy said as they stopped in a crowded and narrow street filled with bustling Chinese merchants and their customers.

To Longarm the two-story brick building painted emerald green appeared no different than any other of the hundreds of small shops and residences that were crowded into the four-square-block area that was Denver's Chinatown. There wasn't even an address posted on the outside of this green building, and its dirty front window was shuttered and unlettered.

Longarm had thought they were going to see someone rich and powerful who would live or do business out of a very impressive building. "Are you sure this is the place?" he asked.

"Of course I'm sure," The Gypsy replied, opening the door into a room that was filled with old Chinese men sitting around drinking tea and nibbling on cakes and fortune cookies. On shelves about three feet off the ground and ringing the room, there were cages filled with noisy rats, ferrets, mice, and even a few snakes that were unlike anything to be found in the American West. On a few of the shelves, Longarm also saw eels and sea creatures floating in glass aquariums or staring back at him with dead eyes.

The elderly Chinese men were startled by The Gypsy's appearance, or perhaps it was the sight of Longarm, so tall and wide shouldered. Whatever it was, they fell into a respectful silence. A very tiny Chinese woman appeared through beaded curtains and smiled at The Gypsy, then bowed to Longarm, who returned the bow. This caused some muted giggling among the older men, which quickly ended when Longarm turned and gave them a piercing stare.

"This way," The Gypsy said, following the woman through the beaded curtains into a dimly lit room filled with vials, packets, boxes, and jars containing things that

109

Longarm could not even imagine. In several of the larger jars, he did see pig's feet and immense insects suspended in a pale greenish liquid that made his flesh crawl.

The little Chinese woman bowed again and vanished behind a barrel containing some rather terrible-smelling fluids.

"What now?" Longarm whispered, wishing there was more light in the little room so that he could see better. The only illumination was provided by about half-a-dozen pumpkin-shaped paper lanterns that looked as if they could ignite and create an inferno without even the slightest aid of a breeze.

"Chu Ling will be here in a moment," The Gypsy said under her breath.

"Is that *opium* that I smell?"

The Gypsy leaned close to Longarm and said, "Custis, please believe me that it would be far better if you just remained silent and let me ask the questions. Otherwise, we may insult Chu Ling and learn nothing."

"Sure," Longarm said, feeling as if people were watching him through holes in the wall. "But I don't much like it here. Is this where you come to visit?"

"Same house, but upstairs there is a room with beds and incense and nice things to turn your mind toward."

Longarm didn't want to see the upstairs room any more than he was enjoying being in this dim and crowded space filled with strange concoctions and assorted oddities.

"So we just wait here?" Longarm asked impatiently.

"Yes. But Chu Ling won't keep us waiting long. That would be very impolite."

Longarm kept looking around and said, "This is the most amazing collection of . . . of oddball *stuff* I've ever seen."

"All of it has value and a specific purpose."

"There must be a thousand little paper and wooden boxes," Longarm said, craning his neck all around. "How would anyone remember what they all contained?"

"Chu Ling and his wife know what's in every box right down to the exact mixtures of compounds and medicines."

"That's what all this is . . . medicine?" Longarm asked with disbelief.

The Gypsy nodded. "There are cures in this room that our own civilization will be trying to find for the next century."

"You really believe in all this, don't you," Longarm said looking into her beautiful face.

"Custis, believe it or not, you would too if you were here long enough to learn even a few of the Orient's secrets."

"Well," Longarm said, "I don't want to be here. This place gives me the creeps."

"Don't say that to Chu Ling," The Gypsy cautioned, "or this visit will have been a complete waste of time and I will not be welcomed back again."

Longarm was about to say something else, but suddenly a very ancient man came through the door and he wore what Longarm thought resembled a woman's flowered dress and white sandals. His hair was silver and long like his beard. His deeply wrinkled face seemed to have been cut out of a block of chipped ice and bore no expression. Yet, the old man had the most amazingly clear eyes that Longarm had ever seen, and they were now fixed on his face, as pure and direct as a shaft of moonlight passing through a white cloud.

Even more amazing was when The Gypsy began to speak to the man in Chinese. Longarm's eyes widened a little and when he realized that his jaw had dropped, he closed his mouth and pretended to take a great interest in an aquarium filled with fish and octopuses. Actually, he had never seen octopuses before, and they were extremely fascinating as their tentacles groped around the inside of their glass prison. Then a small yellow fish swam by, and Longarm saw one of the tentacles grab the fish, which disappeared into the octopus, although Longarm could not determine exactly how or where it vanished.

"Custis, this is Chu Ling," The Gypsy said, breaking him out of his reverie. "I told him about the white powder that you described and he asked if you had a sample."

"Yes," Longarm said, grateful that he had kept some of the strange powder in a small brown envelope, which he now removed from his coat pocket and unfolded. "Here it is, Mr. Ling."

The Chinaman seemed to be looking straight into Longarm's head as he took the envelope and then bent low to first smell, then taste the powder.

"Careful," Longarm said. "I think it might be very deadly poison."

The old man's nose wrinkled just slightly, and then he refolded the paper and gave it back to Longarm while speaking in rapid Chinese to The Gypsy. It was quite a lengthy conversation, and if it had not been for the octopuses moving around in the aquarium stalking fish, Longarm would have become impatient.

Suddenly, Chu Ling bowed to The Gypsy and then to Longarm, and slowly revolved around in his pure white sandals and vanished like mist.

"What?" Longarm asked.

"He told me what you wanted to know. We must leave a donation at the door and leave here at once."

"I've only got about three dollars in my wallet," Longarm said. "I didn't know we had to *pay* the old man."

"Wisdom given as knowledge is always worthy of payment. And don't worry, I have the hundred dollars."

"A hundred dollars!" Longarm exclaimed. "What . . ."

112

"Shhhh!" The Gypsy said, looking annoyed. "Anything less than a hundred dollars would be an insult. And besides, the information that I just received is worth far more than that."

"It's your money," Longarm grumbled. "But I wouldn't pay a man one hundred dollars if he could tell me the day and manner of my death."

"Neither would I," The Gypsy said as the old woman appeared to bow and then lead them back outside. Longarm heard the door lock snap shut behind them.

Once in the crowded streets again, Longarm was on fire to ask what The Gypsy had learned from Chu Ling. However, she wouldn't speak about it until they were out of Chinatown and back in her own residential neighborhood.

But when she did finally tell him, it was worth every penny of the one hundred dollars.

Chapter 17

"The powder," she said, "is an extract from the roots of a plant grown only in a remote region of Mongolia and it is as we suspected a *very* deadly poison. When I told Chu Ling that Chief Muldoon had survived the poison, he said that the chief must have been on other drugs that countered the poison, or else he was part divine."

"Maybe the former," Longarm said skeptically, "but as much as I like and admire Chief Muldoon, he sure isn't divine. Did Chu Ling admit giving or selling this deadly Mongolian-root poison to Abby?"

"Of course not. He has some of it, but it is for the killing of . . . well, things he makes into medicine."

"Then we don't know who . . ."

"He says that the powder was bought from a Chinese man named Hasson Wong."

"How does he know that?"

The Gypsy smiled. "Chu Ling knows everything that happens in Chinatown, and he said that Hasson Wong is a very bad Chinaman."

"All right," Longarm said, a little disappointed. "Then I

guess we go see this Hasson Wong and ask him who he sold the poison to."

"No," The Gypsy said, "Hasson Wong will tell Chu Ling, who will send a man to tell us . . . for a price."

"How much?" Longarm asked.

"One hundred dollars."

Longarm stopped in his tracks. "That's ridiculous. If we pay Wong to tell us who he sold the poison to, then it wouldn't stand up in court. It would be like bribing a witness."

"There is no other way," The Gypsy said. "And besides, I have the money and I want to know."

Longarm shook his head. "How would you know that the name that Wong gives us is really the name of the murderer? For a hundred dollars, I'm sure that old Hasson Wong can come up with about anyone's name."

"He probably would," The Gypsy said, "except that Chu Ling will make sure that he tells us the truth."

Longarm wasn't satisfied with that answer, and yet he felt he was coming up against a stone wall. "So you're telling me that Chu Ling is going to put some muscle on this Hasson Wong fella?"

"Let me put it this way, Custis. If Hasson Wong takes my money and gives us a false name, he will be insulting Chu Ling and that will cause a war between their tongs. And it would be a war that Hasson would lose."

Longarm was having a tough time believing that the little old fella in the dress and white sandals would have the power to hurt anyone. He had appeared so gentle and wise that he seemed like an ancient mystic or scholar rather than the leader of a Chinese gang who would kill an enemy simply because he lied.

"Look," Longarm said. "I believe it that the white powder is a deadly poison from Mongolia. I really do. But that doesn't help us much. We need someone that will tell us who *bought* the medicine."

The Gypsy smiled and said, "We'll have the name to-night. And even more, we'll be told when and where the next meeting is between Hasson Wong and the poisoner."

"We will?"

"Yes. That is what the hundred dollars bought us."

"Then you were right," Longarm said, "it was worth it. All I have to do is to arrest this person with the poison and haul him off to jail. The Denver police will soon have a confession from Abby."

"I doubt that it is Abby buying the poison."

Longarm was caught off guard. "You think—"

"Hasson Wong would not deal with a white woman. He would sell the poison to an intermediary, who would then deliver it to Miss McCall, no doubt doubling the price."

"I see," Longarm said, trying to hide his disappointment. "Things never work out as simple and easy as we hope, do they."

"No," The Gypsy agreed, "but at least we're nearing the end of this deadly puzzle."

"I sure hope so," Longarm said. "Because I'm thinking that Abby McCall is going to run anytime now. And if she does, she'll be doubly hard to catch and prosecute."

"Let's trust my friend Chu Ling. He'll make sure that we have our answers."

"Where are we supposed to be when the answer comes?"

"Back in Chinatown."

"I was afraid you'd say that," Longarm replied. "Because that place is dangerous and I don't entirely trust what will happen there."

He thought that The Gypsy would counter his words or at least reassure him that he was mistaken . . . but she didn't.

• • •

It was midnight as Longarm and The Gypsy stood waiting nervously on a busy street corner in Denver's Chinatown. There were street vendors selling everything from live chickens to small, whining dogs. Longarm wondered if the dogs were to become pets or were doomed to become a dinnertime delicacy. Old men and young stood in small groups talking so fast and loud that Longarm did not understand how they could be heard considering the general din.

"Don't these people ever sleep?" Longarm asked, amazed at all the activity that was going on in Chinatown at this late hour when the rest of Denver was nearly silent.

"They like to do business and to socialize in the late hours," The Gypsy explained. "Custis, you have to understand the Chinese have a very different concept of time than we do."

"I guess so," Longarm agreed. "I just wish Chu Ling's secret messenger would arrive and tell us who bought that rare Mongolian poison from Hasson Wong."

"Be patient. We'll have our answer soon enough."

Longarm was *not* patient. He was standing on a dark corner in Chinatown where he and The Gypsy stood out like sore thumbs. True to their culture, the Chinese were polite people and not inclined to stare, but they couldn't help but do so when they passed the tall Caucasian couple.

It was about twenty minutes later when Longarm saw a small Chinese man dressed in a black smock and sandals appear from behind a building and then look furtively about in all directions. Without actually acknowledging Longarm or The Gypsy, the Chinaman started toward them moving quickly.

"That must be him," Longarm said, stepping forward. "That must be our mysterious messenger."

Before The Gypsy could answer, three other Chinamen

also dressed in black came out of nowhere to swarm over the messenger. Longarm let out a shout of warning and began to run toward the men, but he was too late. The messenger was knocked sprawling and then was swarmed over while being repeatedly stabbed by the trio of assassins.

Longarm drew his gun and shouted, "Stop!"

The three men each buried their knives into the fallen man sent by Chu Ling one last time, and then they turned and attacked Longarm with shrill, unnerving screams.

Longarm's first shot struck the leader of the murderers square in the chest and stopped him in his tracks, but with unbelievable determination and perhaps some kind of chemical help, the man recovered and staggered forward raising his knife and screaming even louder. Longarm fired at the other two attackers and hit them both. Like the first, they slowed, yet did not stop coming with their bloody knives held out in front of them and screams still on their foaming lips.

The first wounded Chinaman closed with Longarm, who jammed his gun up against him and blew a hole in his belly, and then tossed him aside as the other two wounded Chinamen dropped Longarm to the pavement with swift kicks to the sides of his knees. One of the Chinese assassins raised his knife and tried to drive it into Longarm's chest, but Longarm was fortunate enough to grab the crazed man's wrist. He twisted it so hard that bone snapped. The knife dropped from the man's grip, and Longarm snatched it up and buried it in the Chinaman's neck.

The Gypsy shot the third Chinaman, who would probably have managed to slit Longarm's throat as he tried to roll free of the second Chinaman. She fired two shots into the assassin's head, and then grabbed his body and pulled it free so that Longarm could climb to his feet.

Suddenly, the street was empty and silent. No more chattering street vendors and no more clusters of Chinese discussing whatever there was to discuss.

Longarm swayed on his feet and was covered with blood, but fortunately it was not his own. The three assassins were dead, and the messenger was lying in an expanding pool of blood not twenty feet away.

Longarm staggered over to Chu Ling's messenger and saw that there was a small white envelope in his fist. Longarm took the blood-soaked envelope from the messenger's fingers.

"Open it," The Gypsy ordered, her gun still up and ready in case Hasson Wong had sent any more killers.

Longarm tore open the envelope and read the single word neatly written inside: *Killman.*

"Who is Killman?" Longarm asked, turning to the woman beside him.

"He's a hired killer. A silent, deadly assassin that few have ever seen face to face." The Gypsy said, lowering her gun slowly. "Killman is someone that *anyone* would or should fear."

Longarm had never heard of this man. "Do you think that Killman is the poisoner?"

"I would but he's . . . he's *dead.*"

Longarm saw real fear creep into The Gypsy's eyes. And although he had a hundred more questions to ask, he knew that this was not the time or the place.

"Let's get out of here," she said, plainly frightened. "Custis, are you still carrying that packet of Mongolian poison?"

"Yes." Longarm patted his coat. "It's fine."

But The Gypsy disagreed. "It'll be far more secure in my big home safe. I don't want it falling into the wrong hands and killing any more people."

"Good idea," Longarm said as The Gypsy allowed him to remove the small pistol from her clenched fist. Then, she gave him her arm and they left Chinatown and four dead men lying on a nameless and dimly lit street.

And for all the blood and death, they had but a single name. *Killman*.

Chapter 18

It wasn't until they were back at The Gypsy's home and had locked the deadly white powder up in her large safe that Longarm poured them both stiff drinks and said, "Tell me everything you know about Killman."

"I'm afraid that I can't tell you much at all," she admitted. "I do know that he's an underworld figure said to originally hail from New York City. He was the head of some gang back there and got his reputation as a ruthless killer. He was caught, tried, and convicted of multiple murders, but Killman's gang staged his bloody breakout from prison only a few days before his scheduled execution. After that, he left the East and went to California. Soon, he was back to his old ways and more ruthless than ever."

"What is his specialty?"

"Torture, murder, and extortion for hire. It is said that he lived for a while in San Francisco and was protected by a powerful Chinese tong."

The Gypsy shrugged her shoulders and took a deep drink. "I don't know if that is true or not. But I do know that Killman became so notorious in San Francisco's Waterfront District that the local authorities finally had to trap and then arrest him. Several of their policemen were shot in the capture, and Killman was badly wounded. But he was captured at last, and all of San Francisco breathed a little bit easier when Killman was sentenced to die."

"But again he escaped?" Longarm asked.

"This is the troubling part that I don't really understand. According to the San Francisco newspapers, Killman avoided a public hanging because he managed to leap out through the window of a four-story police building and land on the street below."

Longarm lit a cigar and exhaled the smoke as he considered this news. "Four stories is quite a height. If the man landed face-first, he wouldn't be recognizable because his facial features would resemble a ripe red grape crushed against concrete."

"That's a very graphic description," The Gypsy said, shivering slightly. "So you're implying that maybe it wasn't Killman who committed suicide by leaping to his death."

Longarm shrugged. "I'm just fishing. Do you have any better ideas?"

"No. In fact, I don't have any ideas at all."

"How," Longarm asked, "will your friend old Chu Ling take this turn of events and the killing of his personal messenger?"

She did not hesitate. "Not at all well. He'll know that Hasson Wong betrayed him and will kill the man."

Longarm snapped his fingers. "Just like that?"

"Almost. Except my guess is that Hasson Wong will suffer a very slow and terrible death."

"Will you tell Chu Ling that the name given to us by his messenger was Killman?"

"Chu Ling will already know that name by now."

Longarm steepled his long fingers. "So what is our next move?"

"To stay alive," The Gypsy said, tossing down her drink and pouring another. "Just to stay alive until Hasson Wong is dead and his tong is either driven from Denver or eliminated. After I get word of that, then we go back to Chu Ling and see if he can help you find Killman."

"I also intend to find out if Killman is the one that bought the poison and gave it to Miss Abby McCall," Longarm added.

"Yes, that too."

Longarm looked down at his hands and saw dried blood caked under his fingernails that he had missed when he'd first washed his hands at The Gypsy's house. He suddenly felt very tired. "I need to take a bath and then get some sleep."

"You can use my bath."

"No," Longarm said, "I'd like to go back to my apartment. I need some time to think about all this and I need a fresh change of clothes and a shave."

"If you go, you had better watch your backside," The Gypsy warned. "And I mean really watch it closely until I get word from Chu Ling that Hasson Wong and his men have been eliminated."

"I'm good at watching my back," Longarm told her, forcing a tired smile. "But thanks anyway for the warning. I'll come back here tomorrow and we'll wait to hear from Chu Ling. How about I arrive here about noon?"

"That would be fine," she said. "I should have word about Hasson's death by then."

"The Chinese take care of business that quickly, huh?"

"They have the reputation of being a very patient people," The Gypsy told him. "But when it comes to revenge, there are none quicker."

"I would have liked to have met this Hasson Wong," Longarm told her as he finished his drink and prepared to leave.

"No, you wouldn't have," she replied. "Trust me on that."

Longarm went home and took a bath, then slept for nine hours. When he awoke, it was eleven o'clock in the morning and he had trouble coming fully awake, so he drank an extra cup of coffee as he prepared a hasty breakfast, then shaved and dressed. His striped yellow cat, Tom, appeared in his window complaining about not having been fed in a few days.

"Sorry about that," Longarm said, digging out some meat from his icebox and a bottle of milk that had curdled.

Tom devoured the old meat and lapped up the bad milk. He licked his chops and started to purr as he climbed onto Longarm's bed, stretched, and then prepared to take a long nap.

"Make yourself right at home," Longarm said with a yawn and no small amount of envy.

While sleeping, Longarm had suffered nightmares about Chinese assassins, and even now in the cold light of day, he still could smell their strange scent and recall how close he had come to being hacked to death on that dark and nameless street somewhere deep in Chinatown.

And this man Killman, what kind of monster might he be? Longarm knew that sometimes the worst murderers and criminals looked like physicians or university professors. On the other hand, sometimes you could just see the evil in their eyes that could never be disguised.

"Guard the fort, Tom," Longarm called out as he left his apartment strapping on his sidearm.

It was a nice but breezy day as Longarm headed downtown and then out to see The Gypsy. As he walked along, he kept very aware of everyone who passed close by him and wondered if this Killman was a big or a small man. And what kind of a name was that anyway? Killman. Too coincidental to be his real name, and so it was almost certainly an alias. And finally, Longarm couldn't help but wonder if this mysterious assassin named Killman, late of New York City and then San Francisco, had been recruited by the late Lieutenant Gavin Kelly, who'd then hooked the assassin up with Miss Abby McCall.

One thing for sure. If Abby was about to inherit the Stanton fortune and this Killman fella was really alive and in Denver, Longarm could almost bet that Abby's young life was in grave jeopardy just as soon as the inheritance passed to her. Someone like Killman wouldn't be content to take peanuts for pay . . . hell, no . . . he'd want the lion's share of the Stanton estate.

Longarm wondered if Abby was smart enough to know that when you ran with a jackal, you could expect it to eventually rip out your throat, then roar in pure primal pleasure.

Chapter 19

Longarm pulled his Ingersoll pocket watch from his vest and consulted the time. It was 12:45 P.M., so he was going to be a little bit late for his promised noon appointment by the time he arrived at The Gypsy's house. Stepping up his pace, he hurried down the street wondering if the woman had been able to find out any more information about Killman. And if Hasson Wong was the one who had tried to have them murdered last evening, then Longarm didn't care a bit if Chu Ling and his tong eliminated Wong and his Chinese cutthroats.

It was an amazing yet true fact that the Chinese in the Western cities were almost always a society and law unto themselves. Frontier marshals did not interfere with the ostracized Chinese, and turned their heads when the tongs or individual Chinese fought their gruesome battles. On more than one occasion while in some Western town, Longarm had heard lawmen say, "The Chinamen are just a bunch of dirty yellow monkeys. Let 'em kill each other off and good riddance to my town. I'm a marshal to protect the white Americans and I don't even consider them humans."

But the Chinese *were* humans, although very different in

their ways and outlook from all other Americans. And while they were the most secretive and clannish people Longarm had ever come across, it was obvious that they lived, bred, prospered, suffered, and died just like the rest of the population.

When Longarm arrived at The Gypsy's opulent home, he repeatedly knocked on her massive front door, but there was no answer. Thinking that the wealthy woman might be in the back tending to her flower garden or taking tea in the fine morning air, Longarm went through a side gate to find her.

He found her all right, but The Gypsy was lying in her well-tended garden with a Chinese sword buried in her chest nearly to its hilt. She wore a flowered and lacy night-gown that was now ripped by the blade of the sword and sodden with her blood.

"Gawdamn!" Longarm choked as he knelt beside the woman who had been his trusted friend.

Judging from the body and blood, The Gypsy had not been killed more than an hour earlier, a fact that caused Longarm a great deal of guilt. If he had been here at noon as promised, then he might have been able to save the woman.

A quick look around revealed that The Gypsy had put up a valiant fight for her life. Her carefully tended flower beds were in ruin, flattened and broken as a result of the life-and-death struggle she'd waged. An ornate marble statue had been knocked over and broken; a heavy brass bird feeder was spilled over on its side and its contents were still not dry. An ornate wrought-iron table and two chairs were spilled onto a walkway, and a fragile teapot and cup were shattered and trampled.

"The murdering bastard caught her here," Longarm said to himself, "unarmed and unprotected, enjoying her tea and her flowers and the morning sunshine."

Longarm studied the battered and mutilated lady while fighting back a dark rage. "You didn't deserve this," he whispered, "and you'd still be alive if I hadn't dragged you into these murders."

The Gypsy's face was purplish and her nose had no doubt been broken. Despite all the physical damage, Longarm thought her still exceptionally beautiful. He saw that several of her fingernails had been ripped off and that under others there were pieces of bloody flesh.

Killman's flesh and blood?

Longarm had no way of knowing if Killman had been the one that had so brutally murdered The Gypsy. But he was dead certain of one thing. He would find out no matter how long it took or how far he had to travel. Up until this moment, Killman had been merely the name of an evil man who needed to be stopped. But now as he stared down at The Gypsy's body, Longarm felt a powerful and very personal hatred enter his mind and body.

"If he did this to you, then a hangman's rope is too good an end for the man," Longarm vowed. "For the first time ever, I will make sure he dies slow and screaming."

With tears in his eyes, Longarm turned away and entered the big house, where he found a pretty quilt, which he then took outside to cover the body. Longarm was careful not to disturb anything outside, knowing that the Denver police would want to examine an undisturbed crime scene. "Did he catch you in the house or just as you were coming outside?" Longarm asked out loud.

He went inside and looked around the room, noticing blood on the carpet and more evidence of a struggle. As he

131

followed the blood spatters, he went down the hall to the library where The Gypsy often spent her leisure hours and where her safe was located.

Its massive door was hanging wide open. Longarm hurried over and saw that it was empty and there was drying blood on the dial. Only last night he'd seen The Gypsy use this dial to open the massive safe where she kept stacks of currency as well as her most valuable jewelry. Now, the safe was as empty as a bare cupboard shelf and in addition to the cash and jewelry, Longarm saw that the Mongolian poison was missing.

He stood up and thought for a moment about this fact, and realized that it only confirmed what he had already known . . . this was not a common burglary turned murder. This tragedy was a well-planned strike by someone who badly wanted both money and the poison in order to murder again and again.

A hard chill passed down Longarm's spine. What it meant was that the murderer, probably the one named Killman, was back in the poisoning business. And, if he knew about The Gypsy's involvement, he'd know about Longarm's as well.

Maybe I'm next, Longarm thought, suddenly feeling anxious. *Maybe he won't try to simply stab or shoot me, but instead find a way to slip the poison into my food or drink.*

And he could do that in a hundred everyday places. My apartment. My favorite saloon. From a smiling Denver street vendor selling me a liquid refreshment on my way home from the office. Or at my favorite market, just before I pick up a bottle of cool milk placed at the front of the grocer's shelf. There is almost no way that I can know or predict where he might find me vulnerable and use that tasteless, odorless poison.

Right then Longarm made a conscious decision. He *had* to find Killman before the man found him. Had to!

But how? Longarm knew of only two people who might be able to give him a lead. One was Chu Ling, who might help him because Chu Ling had considered The Gypsy a trusted friend and he would be anxious for revenge. And the other person was Miss Abby McCall, who was probably the first one to bring Killman into this twisted and murderous affair all caused by the Stanton estate inheritance.

Longarm did not know where to find Abby or even if she was still alive. But he did know where to find Chu Ling . . . at least he thought he could find that little door in Chinatown.

So he would go to Chu Ling first to communicate with the old Chinaman and get him to find Killman and do whatever he wished and damn the courts and the established local or federal law.

Failing that, Longarm would turn this town upside down just in case Abby McCall was still here and still alive.

Chapter 20

Remembering that Chu Ling did business in the midnight hours, Longarm went back into Chinatown late that night. After a few wrong turns, he managed to find the tong leader's place of business because of its green door. Longarm knocked and waited, not sure what to expect. When the door finally opened, he stood face-to-face with the biggest Chinaman he had ever beheld. The man was at least six and a half feet tall and would weigh over three hundred pounds. He was probably in his mid-twenties, but he might have been ten years older.

The Chinese giant was dressed in a black silk tunic, pants, and thick leather sandals. His massive head was closely shaved except for a long, braided queue, and he wore a sword at his belt and held a curved dagger in his ham-sized fist. He was powerfully built, with dark and piercing eyes. Rarely had Longarm met such an intimidating man, and he almost took a backward step and made an impulsive grab for his six-gun.

Instead, he steadied himself and said to the impassive giant guarding Chu Ling's house, "I am a friend of The Gypsy. The Gypsy was a friend of Chu Ling. I wish to tell

Chu Ling about her death and ask for his help in finding her killer."

Longarm realized that his speech was stiff and unnaturally long. The impassive and imposing Chinaman gave no hint that he was even listening, much less that he understood English. But when Longarm was finished, the guard pushed Longarm aside, then studied the street to make sure that there were no other visitors. Satisfied that no danger lurked outside the door of his master, he pointed at Longarm's Colt revolver and made it clear that he wanted possession of the weapon.

Longarm was not in the habit of turning his gun over to anyone. He was a deputy U.S. marshal and he carried a badge as proof of his authority. So he could have shook his head and let the guard know that he wasn't going to give over his weapon, but he realized that mistake would either get him killed or sent away.

"All right," he agreed, handing over the Colt revolver, knowing that, if worse came to worst, he still had his little hideout derringer attached to his watch fob. "Now take me to Chu Ling."

"As you wish," the giant said, surprising Longarm.

The guard then escorted Longarm into the same room that they had entered the night before with The Gypsy. When the same gathering of old Chinamen smoking opium slowly turned to look at him, Longarm thought he saw hostility and distrust this night.

"Good evening," he said to the group, offering them a slight bow of respect.

Not one of them acknowledged his greeting. The giant grunted something unintelligible, and then Longarm was led past the gathering and down several narrow corridors that were scented with flowers and opium.

When he entered the room where Chu Ling was reposing

on a large and ornately carved bed with many pillows and two lovely Chinese girls, Longarm wasn't sure what to do or to say. The guard stepped directly behind him, and Longarm could feel the man's dark and dangerous presence.

"Good evening, Chu Ling," Longarm said, bowing slightly. "I have come with very bad news about The Gypsy."

The girls were obviously twins, and they sat up straight and then climbed off Chu Ling's bed to hover near their master. They were so young and beautiful that Longarm was momentarily distracted by the pair. But he quickly regained his focus.

"Chu Ling, our friend was murdered at her house this morning, and then robbed not only of her jewelry and money, but also of the deadly white Mongolian poison."

Chu Ling said something in a rather harsh tone to the lovely young girls, who bowed deeply to him and then hurried from the room. The old Chinese warlord then gave a second order, and the guard behind Longarm disappeared without a sound. Longarm only knew this because he dared to glance over his left shoulder.

"I am very sad to hear of this," Chu Ling said in rather shrill but understandable English. "The Gypsy was an honorable woman whose company I greatly enjoyed."

"She was stabbed to death," Longarm said, unable to hide his bitterness and anger, "but she fought hard for her life. I thought you might know who did this thing and help me find him."

Chu Ling studied Longarm for a moment. "Then you would arrest this man and take him to jail."

"Yes."

"And have what your people call a *trial*."

"Yes, but . . ."

"And maybe this man who killed our lady friend, he has

a very good . . . what do you call these persons of learning of the law?"

"A lawyer."

"Yes, a good lawyer, and this man with his fingers dripping with The Gypsy's blood is perhaps found not guilty and freed."

"It could happen," Longarm admitted, "but I'm hoping that—"

"Your hopes are of no matter to me," Chu Ling interrupted, with a sudden show of controlled but unmistakable anger. "This man who killed our friend is clever and dangerous. He will not be caught and sent to prison, and he will never be hanged."

Longarm wasn't sure how to respond, so he remained silent. Apparently, this was the right thing to do, because Chu Ling visibly relaxed, then motioned him forward and said, "I am told that you are called Longarm."

"I have been called that."

"Because you are the white man's law and it has a long reach."

Longarm had no idea where this conversation was leading and so he said, "I guess that's the way it is. I need to find this man who killed The Gypsy and many others because I think he will try to kill me next. Maybe with the same poison that he has already used right here in Denver."

Chu Ling nodded in agreement. "Yes, this is possible."

"Who is Killman and where can I find him?"

"He is gone from our city," Chu Ling said, his eyes turning inward. "But maybe not far."

"I must find him quickly."

"I will find him for you," Chu Ling replied. "And this man Killman will poison no more. He will die slowly and screaming for mercy, but he gave no mercy to our friend and he will receive none."

"Chu Ling, this is a matter for the law."

"Will you kill him?"

"If necessary," Longarm answered.

"And will you kill the woman, too?"

"Are you speaking of Miss Abby McCall?"

"Of course," Chu Ling said.

"I will arrest them both and they will stand trial."

Chu Ling shook his head with obvious disappointment. "Better I find these people."

"No!" Longarm saw Chu Ling's reaction to his outburst and immediately knew that he had made a mistake. "I'm sorry," he said quickly. "But I have to do this myself."

"If you try, they will kill you and then both escape . . . even from my reach."

Longarm felt that this conversation had reached an impasse. "Does that mean you will not help me?"

"I will help."

Before Longarm could form a response, Chu Ling clapped his hands and the huge guard reappeared. For a moment, Chu Ling spoke in rapid Chinese to the giant, and then he clapped his hands once and the man again vanished.

"What did you say to him?" Longarm asked.

"I told him to protect you and then take the lives of Killman and Miss McCall."

"I must refuse his help," Longarm said firmly. "I won't have an assassin hanging over my shoulder. I have my own way of doing things and I will not fail."

"I have made my decision," Chu Ling said just as if he hadn't heard a single word of Longarm's protest.

"What is your man's name?"

"His name is unimportant," Chu Ling answered. "He is my slave. I took him as a boy and he has been with me all his life. You can trust him. He will protect you with *his* life."

139

"But I don't *need* his protection."

"You are wrong, Longarm," Chu Ling said, suddenly weary of this conversation. "Now go because I need to make an offering for the death of my friend The Gypsy."

"Your slave took my gun. I want it back right now."

"When you go outside, he will be waiting for you and you will have the gun back then."

"I can't allow your man to murder Abby McCall and this Killman," Longarm said. "I want you to understand this because it is important."

Chu Ling dismissed those words with a wave of his hand. "I have given my orders to him and he will kill them both."

"Don't you understand? If your man murders them, then I will have to arrest him and he could be hanged."

"It is of no matter to me," Chu Ling said. "Go."

Longarm had never before been so summarily dismissed. He knew that if he tried to argue with Chu Ling, it would only anger the old Chinaman, and perhaps even get Longarm killed right here and now. He did have that derringer, but that would not get him back outside in one piece.

To hell with it, Longarm decided. Once he got his pistol back outside, he would give the giant the slip and then go about his business. It seemed painfully obvious now that it had been a waste of time to solicit Chu Ling's help.

Chapter 21

The huge slave was waiting outside, and he carried a large canvas cloth bag slung over his muscular shoulder. Longarm had no idea of the bag's contents, but he did appreciate it when the giant returned his Colt revolver.

"Listen," Longarm said, glancing up and down the dark but still busy streets of Chinatown. "I don't want your help. I told Chu Ling that, but he insisted you should accompany me in finding this man named Killman and perhaps also Miss Abby McCall."

"I know where to find them," the giant said.

"You do?"

He nodded.

Longarm said, "Then why don't you just tell me and I'll go arrest the pair and that will be the end of it. Chu Ling doesn't have to know that you weren't with me."

"Chu Ling knows everything," the giant answered matter-of-factly. "If I disobey, then my sisters will die."

Longarm shook his head. "What are you talking about?"

But the man shook his head. "Follow me."

Longarm had no choice but to follow, and despite the

fact that he had long legs, he was hard pressed to keep up with the towering slave whose stride had to cover five feet.

"I'm going to arrest them," Longarm said when they reached the outskirts of Chinatown. "And I want you to promise me that you won't interfere."

"I will kill them and then you can arrest *me*."

Longarm had never met anyone either so stupid or so obstinate. "Can't you get it through your thick head that I don't want to arrest you?"

The giant said nothing, prompting Longarm to ask, "What's your name?"

"Ishir," the man said. "And my family is *not* Chinese. We are Mongols who raised sheep in the Gobi Desert. My father was killed by Chinese and our sheep were stolen. My mother died in China and my little sisters became slaves."

"Was this done by Chu Ling's people?"

The Mongol shook his head. "No. By slave traders from the city of Baotou near the Yellow River. When I was ten years old, I was sold to Chu Ling's family and trained to fight in the city of Macao on the South China Sea. It was from that port that I and my sisters were sent first to San Francisco, then on foot all the way to Denver."

"You were sent to this city to always protect Chu Ling?"

"Yes. To the death. If I fail, my sisters will be put to death."

"Were those your sisters that I saw with Chu Ling?"

"Enough talk!" the Mongol said, telling Longarm that it *was* his sisters that he had just seen resting on Chu Ling's bed.

Longarm had to hurry after the man. "Where are we going?"

"To the mountains."

"Then we'll need horses."

But the Mongol giant wasn't even listening as he hurried west through the night.

Longarm had no choice but to hurry after Ishir because he alone had been told by Chu Ling where Killman and Abby were hiding. But many hours later, when the first streaks of dawn were beginning to touch the crown of the Rocky Mountains, Longarm knew that he could not possibly keep pace on foot with the Mongol, who never rested or showed any sign of fatigue.

"Stop!" Longarm ordered.

Ishir halted on a rugged foothill and turned to Longarm, folding his arms across his chest to indicate his displeasure. It really galled Longarm to see that the Mongol hadn't even broken a sweat despite the fact that Denver was far below and many miles behind.

"I don't know how far we're supposed to go like this, but I'm not going another step up this mountain until I have some answers."

Ishir looked to the east and the rising sun. He stood very still before he finally glanced down at Longarm and said, "Black Canyon."

"Are you crazy! That's a good twenty miles farther."

Ishir merely shrugged and started to turn and continue up the mountain, but Longarm drew his gun and cocked the hammer. "Ishir, you had better stop or I'll shoot."

The Mongol turned back again. "If you kill me, then you kill my sisters and the ones you seek to bring to justice will escape."

"Then maybe I'll just shoot you in the knee and then you'll have no choice but to tell me where to find Killman and Abby."

Ishir shook his head.

So there it was, and Longarm realized that he held no

cards in this game. If he wounded Ishir, the man would not speak and might even bleed to death. If that happened, the sisters would die and the ones that he sought to arrest would escape, unless he got lucky and found them in Black Canyon.

Swearing under his breath, Longarm holstered his gun and said, "There's a town just up ahead, and these boots I'm wearing were never intended for hiking up mountains. Dammit, Ishir, you might be made of cast iron, but I'm all done in and that's no way for me to come face-to-face with Killman. So I'm asking you, as one reasonable human being to another, that we buy a ride the rest of the way up to Black Canyon. Once there, we rest up a few hours and then we take Killman down together."

Ishir shook his shaved head.

"Why not?" Longarm asked. "If we mess this up, not only will we get killed, but you'll have failed and your sisters will die. Has it occurred to you that Killman might have men protecting him just like you protect Chu Ling? He now has The Gypsy's jewels and money. He could have hired a dozen gunslingers. Do you want those sisters to die because of your stubbornness?"

The Mongol looked down for a moment, and then said, "My sisters are all that I live for."

Longarm heard the pain in the Mongol's voice and knew that he was telling the truth. "Has your master Chu Ling promised to set them free if you succeed in killing this enemy?"

"Yes."

"And," Longarm continued, "has Chu Ling also promised to set *you* free?"

Ishir shook his head. "I will never be freed until my master, Chu Ling, is dead."

"Slavery is outlawed in America. We just fought a war that made it so. I can help you and your sisters break the bond and be freed from Chu Ling. I can help you go some-place where his tong will never find you."

Longarm let that sink in for a moment. "If you take me to where I can find Killman . . . then I'll take some of his money and buy you and your sisters passage to wherever you want to go. San Francisco? New York?"

A faraway look crept into the Mongol's dark eyes and he whispered, "We would go home to the Gobi Desert."

Longarm shook his head with disbelief. "Ishir, are you telling me that you and your sisters really want to return to Mongolia?"

There was a firm dip of the Mongol's chin.

"All right," Longarm said, having no idea how much money it would take to send these people back to a desert halfway around the world. "Ishir, if you hold up your end of this, then you and your sisters will see your homeland again."

The Mongol smiled.

Chapter 22

A huge gold rush had occurred in Black Canyon about twenty years earlier and, for a good decade, the town had boomed as mining operations sprouted up all over the canyon creating immense wealth. Then, almost as suddenly as the boom had begun, it had ended. All the mines went bust and the town emptied overnight. Left in the wake of the departing money and miners was a ghost town where only a few diehards remained, men who could not believe the dream of Black Canyon was dead and gone.

And now, as Longarm and Ishir rode a buckboard up the potholed road into the nearly empty town, the sky was dark with threatening rain.

"Thanks for the lift!" Longarm called as he and Ishir jumped off the back of the wagon bound for a distant and prosperous camp that would no doubt ultimately suffer the same fate as Black Canyon when its ore eventually played out.

"There ain't but one saloon left open," the driver called. "It's the Green Parrot and you can't miss 'er."

Longarm heard the crack of thunder over the high mountains just to their west and saw a gathering storm. He

147

glanced up and down the street and saw just two horses hitched to a supply wagon in front of a vacant building whose front windows were all busted out. With the rising wind, a piece of roofing tin was rattling somewhere nearby like dice in a glass jar.

"Ishir, I remember coming up here and you could hardly move up or down this main street," he told the Mongolian. "This was one of the wildest boom towns I've ever seen and the money flowed from the deep-rock mines like water. But now, it's all gone except for about half the buildings."

The Mongolian said nothing as he stood with his feet wide apart surveying the abandoned mining town.

Longarm checked his gun. "I guess we'll go to the Green Parrot and see what we can find out. Maybe even have a beer for breakfast."

Longarm didn't expect to find Abby McCall or the assassin named Killman walking around the nearly deserted town of Black Canyon. There was nobody walking about except a few old dogs and one old man who asked Longarm if he could have money for whiskey.

"Sure," Longarm said, giving the man a silver dollar in the expectation of asking him about the whereabouts of Abby McCall. "Old-timer, I suppose you've been here for many years and have seen this town go from boom to bust."

"Yep. But it's gonna boom again," the old man promised, his eyes lighting up with the memory of better times long past. "That's why I still own a few buildings here. I could buy more real cheap, but I'm kinda down on my luck. Only a temporary thing, though. This town will come back and so will I."

"I'm sure you will," Longarm said, knowing that would never happen. "I'll bet there's plenty of gold underfoot that was never found."

"There you go! I been sayin' that for years. And by the way, my name is Zack. Old Zack Kendrick."

"Pleased to meet you." Longarm shook the man's hand and said, "By the way, Zack, have you seen a pretty young woman with black hair and dark eyes come into town this past week?"

"Why, you must be talkin' about that rich widow, Mrs. Stanton."

"Yes, I am," Longarm said, sure that he was alluding to Abby McCall.

"Well," the old man said, pointing to a huge mansion overlooking the abandoned town, "you see that big old palace up there clinging to the mountainside with four chimneys pokin' out of the roof?"

"Sure do."

"Mrs. Stanton just showed up late last week and moved into that mansion. It'd been empty nearly eight years."

Longarm studied the mansion, which clung precariously to the cut-out side of a massive slab of granite looming directly to the west of town. Behind the mansion loomed a cliff at least two hundred feet tall, and the only way up to the house was by traveling a narrow, winding road that looked to be half washed away.

"Does Mrs. Stanton ever come down here for supplies or anything?" Longarm asked as thunder and lightning played ever nearer over the peaks.

"Not so far. We're all waiting to see her up close. But she's got a crew up there that work the mine behind the mansion. In its heyday, the mine produced enough silver to pave every street in this town. I wish they'd done it too so I could pick out enough for a few whiskies and some grits. The pickin's is pretty lean up here in this canyon."

"I can see that," Longarm said. "And I wonder how many men are working for the woman."

149

"I think there's three or four," Zack assured him. "And they're hard cases that don't look or act like miners. They come into town most evenings and keep our saloon afloat, but they ain't a bit friendly. I stay clear of 'em for the sake of my health."

The old man scratched his head and stared at the Mongolian. "He don't seem very friendly, either. Is your big friend a Chinaman?"

"Ishir is from Mongolia."

Zack scratched his scraggly gray beard. "Is that near Africa or the Canary Islands?"

"Nope," Longarm answered, "Mongolia is on the other side of the world bordering China. It has a big desert called the Gobi. Ishir and his family raised sheep there and he'd like to go home."

The Mongol seemed to fascinate the old man, who mustered up the courage to ask, "How come your friend wears those black pajamas and has his hair all braided up in a single pigtail?"

"It's just his way," Longarm answered.

The old man rubbed the silver dollar that Longarm had given him and said thoughtfully, "He's big so I wouldn't ever grab that girlish pigtail or try to cut it off. But those hard cases workin' for Mrs. Stanton will probably get after him. If he's your friend, then my advice is that you'd better keep him out of their sight for his own protection."

"Thanks for the warning."

"I'm going to go down and have a drink," Zack said, licking his lips. "You fellas care to join me?"

"I don't mind if we do."

"I ain't sure if the man who owns the Green Parrot will let that Chinaman in to drink."

"I don't want a drink," Ishir said quietly.

"He speaks English!" Zack slapped his pants and created a little cloud of dust. "Well, I'll be damned. I thought he was a mute or only spoke Chinaman language."

"He's no mute or Chinaman," Longarm reminded the old-timer. "Is there anyplace here in town where we can get something to eat?"

"John at the Green Parrot will fry you up some pork and potatoes. Makes good coffee, if that's your pleasure. But I'd recommend the whiskey. He makes it out behind the building and it'll curl your hair for certain."

"I better go for the coffee and breakfast," Longarm said. "Ishir?"

"I am hungry."

"Good," Longarm said. "Then let's go visit the Green Parrot and have some breakfast."

Longarm and Ishir turned and had started to follow Zack up the street when a volley of rifle shots boomed, their sounds melded with the clash of lightning and hammering of nearby thunder. Longarm felt a bullet pluck the sleeve of his arm, and he saw both Zack and Ishir stagger and fall. More bullets filled the street, and Longarm dove headfirst behind an old water trough with splinters digging into his face.

He searched desperately for smoke or a sign of movement that would pinpoint the ambushers, but he saw nothing. Rain began to fall, first a few drops, and then a hard, drenching downpour.

Zack wasn't moving and Longarm could see the blood running out of his head, but Ishir was still alive and trying to drag himself to cover. Longarm cursed at the rain, and then he made a desperate run to grab Ishir's arm and try and pull him behind some cover.

But the ambushers were anticipating that move and Longarm took a slug in the shoulder. He fell heavily beside the Mongolian, and had it not been for the heavy downpour, they'd have been riddled on the ground. A bolt of lightning struck a tree and set it on fire as they both some-how found the strength and will to scrabble to safety bleed-ing heavily.

"Looks like they found us before we found them," Longarm said, clenching his teeth in pain. "Are you going to make it?"

"Yes," Ishir said, but he sounded weak. "I'll live long enough to kill them *all*."

Longarm nodded, and he didn't bother to argue the point. It was clear from this moment on that it was kill or be killed in Black Canyon.

Chapter 23

Longarm pulled Ishir in close behind the horse-watering trough and yelled over the storm, "How bad are you hit?"

"Broken ribs. Maybe worse."

Longarm peered through the driving rain. "We need to get into one of these abandoned buildings and see how much damage we've both suffered. Can you stand up and run for that old store with the broken window?"

"Yes," Ishir gritted.

Longarm looked up at the sky. "If this rain lets up and we're still pinned down here, we're as good as dead. We need to get off this street and into a building quick."

"You're shot, too," Ishir said, noting the blood soaking into the shoulder of Longarm's coat. "How bad?"

"I don't know. But it's my left shoulder so I can still shoot straight. Let's get ready to make a break for that building while the storm is still at its worst."

Ishir grabbed the edge of the trough and pulled himself into a crouch. "I'm ready, but you go first."

"No," Longarm said. "I've got the gun so I'll cover you. Now run!"

Ishir jumped up and ran with amazing speed considering he'd been shot in the side. He didn't try to leap through the broken window, but instead slammed his shoulder into the door and sent it crashing off its hinges with bullets flying around him.

Longarm thought he caught sight of muzzle flashes across the street and up on the roof of a big, two-story brick mercantile building. He fired three times up at the rooftop, then sprinted hard for cover. A bullet clipped his empty holster, nearly tearing it apart. Another bullet creased his Stetson, but by then he was diving into the building.

"How many do you think are up there?" Ishir asked a few moments later as gunfire still boomed from the high roof.

"My guess is two and they're using rifles. Let's take a look at our damage before we do anything foolish."

Ishir raised his black tunic and studied his side. Longarm bent close because the light was poor and said, "I'm going to check this and it might hurt."

Ishir nodded and Longarm ran his finger over the entry wound, and then gently massaged the ribs and felt around behind the giant's muscular back. "The good news," he said to the Mongol, "is that the bullet ricocheted off the ribs and exited without hitting your spine. But the bad news is that there is probably more than one broken rib and you're bleeding pretty badly."

"It isn't important."

"It is if you bleed to death," Longarm said, glancing around the interior of the building until he saw a few pieces of old bolts of calico. "This must have been a dry-goods store. I'll get some of that spoiled yardage and wrap you up tighter than a papoose on a cradle board."

Ishir didn't say anything until that was done, and then

154

he helped Longarm remove his ruined coat. "Hurts like the devil," said Longarm.

Even a quick inspection showed that the bullet had clipped his collarbone, tearing some tissue and maybe even some bone, but he wasn't bleeding profusely.

Several more bullets probed the open door from across the street. "They're still firing down at us from the roof. We can either hole up here until they grow tired of this game or we can try to capture them."

"Let's kill them," Ishir said, drawing a curved knife from his clothing. "I'll do it."

"Dammit, Ishir, I mean to take them alive," Longarm argued. "If we can get at least one of them to talk, we'll both be better off for the information."

When the huge Mongol didn't reply, Longarm grabbed the man by his thick wrist and hissed, "Listen to me! I'm an officer of the law and I want to capture those men alive, if at all possible. This goes way deeper than you and me being fired upon up here in Black Canyon. That might be Killman up there, and I want to see him dance at the end of a hangman's stiff noose."

It was clear that Ishir didn't want to try to "capture" the ambushers. But Longarm's tone of voice made him finally nod his head in reluctant agreement.

"All right," Longarm said, still not trusting the Mongol. "Let's go out the back way. There must be an alley and we can use it to flank those two on the roof. Maybe meet up behind the building and catch them when they come down. And I expect they will come down soon given that they're being drenched and are in danger of being struck by lightning."

Ten minutes later, Longarm was waiting behind the mercantile and staring up at its rooftop. He didn't know where the hell the Mongol was, and he wasn't even sure that the ambushers were still on the roof. Not quite willing to enter the mercantile and try to locate the inner staircase, Longarm decided to give it a few more minutes even though he was wet, bleeding, and feeling as miserable as a drowned dog.

He shivered with a chill and wished he could have a big gulp of whiskey and a cigar. Damn but this rain was falling hard! Longarm tried to move under the lip of the high roof by pressing his back to the wall, but that didn't help because water was cascading down on him in a waterfall.

Where the hell is Ishir! Where is that Mongol giant when you really need him in a pinch?

Suddenly, over the fury of the storm, Longarm heard a high, piercing scream, and then a body was hurled off the rooftop and landed with a sickening *splat* in the mud of the alley behind the mercantile.

He then heard a second scream and a man begging for his life. "No, please!"

Longarm stepped away from the wall of the building and put his hand over his eyes to momentarily shield them from the cascade. What he saw made his jaw drop. Ishir had the second ambusher by his ankles and was dangling him upside down over empty space.

"No, please!" the man hollered, his eyes wide with terror.

"Ishir, don't do it!" Longarm shouted. "Bring him down here!"

For what seemed an eternity, the giant dangled the ambusher, whose arms were windmilling. At last, Ishir pulled the shooter up and they both disappeared.

Longarm found the back door to the mercantile hanging open, probably because the Mongol had already used it minutes earlier. He stepped out of the torrent of rain and leaned up against the wall shivering.

Ishir came down the stairs with his knife held at the

throat of his hostage. The man was nearly hysterical and blubbering incoherently. When he was brought before Longarm, his knees crumpled and he collapsed on the floor. Longarm wasn't used to seeing a hired gunman reduced to such a pathetic state. But then he wasn't used to seeing a man dangled two stories over an alley by his heels, either.

"Stand up straight," Longarm commanded. "You're not hurt . . . yet."

The man wiped snot, tears, and water off his face, then tried to focus on Longarm. "What are you going to do to me?" he asked, voice trembling.

"Depends on what you have to say."

"I've got nothing to say to either of you."

"Ishir," Longarm said, "I guess you should have dropped him from up there on the roof. But now that you're down here, why don't you just slit his damned throat."

"No!" the man cried as Ishir raised his wicked-looking knife. "Oh, Gawd, no!"

"If you want to live, you'd better sing like a canary or your blood will flow like a river," Longarm told him. "You and your friend opened up on us from up on the roof and you wounded us both, so we're not in a mood to be charitable."

The ambusher swallowed hard and then asked, "If I tell you what you want to know, will you let me go?"

"I'm a United States marshal and you're under arrest for attempted murder. That will get you prison time, but you won't be hanged unless you lie or try to escape. Are you understanding me?"

The man nodded his head vigorously.

"Good," Longarm said, glancing deeper into the dusty old building with its rows and rows of empty and overturned shelves. "Let's get someplace where we can sit down and have a good, long chat."

"I don't know anything," the man stammered as Longarm shoved him into the mercantile and then motioned for him to sit.

"So you and your late friend just like to ambush people from rooftops for no other reason than you're killers?"

The man wiped his nose on his sleeve and snorted up snot. He was probably in his mid-twenties, thin and with a pocked face. He had close-set eyes and a pointed jaw with a little goatee, the number of curly hairs you could count on both hands. He had the look of a cornered ferret, and Longarm would have picked him for a dangerous criminal had he seen him standing on any street corner.

"Tell me why you tried to kill us out there," Longarm said. "If you're lying, I'll let the giant cut your throat."

"I thought you said I was under arrest!"

"I did. But given the circumstances and the fact that you and your friend are cold-blooded ambushers, I'm going to suspend the rules and become your judge and jury. If you lie . . . you die."

"Oh, man, please don't talk like that!"

"Then tell us the truth. It's your only chance and I'm not a patient man."

The ambusher's frightened ferret eyes shifted over to Ishir, who still held that curved knife and appeared eager to test its sharpness.

"All right. Burt and I were hired to kill you both."

"By who?" Longarm demanded.

"By . . . by Mrs. Stanton."

"And?"

"By a man named Killman."

"Are they hiding up at that mansion?" Longarm asked.

"She is, but he left a day ago."

"Where did he go?"

"I have no idea."

Longarm glanced at Ishir, who moved closer with his terrible knife.

"Honest, I don't!" the ambusher screamed. "I just work for 'em, that's all. Mrs. Stanton said that you were both trying to rob and kill her. That you were after her fortune and our job was to kill you first."

"Where did Killman go?" Longarm repeated.

"I swear I don't know!"

Longarm glanced over at the Mongol. "See how he bleeds."

"No!" the man screamed as Ishir drew his blade lightly across the man's neck drawing a line of dripping crimson. "No, please don't do it!"

"One more time," Longarm said. "Where did this Killman go?"

"To Denver!"

Longarm waved the Mongol back. "*Where* in Denver?"

"I don't know. They didn't tell me anything, but I overheard Mrs. Stanton tell Killman to go to Denver and finish their business."

"That's it?" Longarm asked.

"That's it. I swear that's all that I heard, on my mother's grave."

Longarm was feeling a little dizzy from the loss of blood and he needed a drink, some rest, and food. He also yearned for dry clothes and a warm, soft bed.

"How many men are up there at the mansion?" Ishir asked.

The ambusher blinked rapidly. It was clear that he was petrified of the Mongol. "Four and Mrs. Stanton. There were seven before Killman, Burt, and me left. So there's only four now . . . and the lady."

"She's no lady," Longarm said without thought. "She's anything but a lady."

"She's rich as a queen," the ambusher said with a hint of defensiveness. "She paid us plenty. More than I ever earned in my life."

"Yeah," Longarm said, mocking the cowardly ambusher. "I'll just bet that she did."

The Mongol must have seen Longarm shivering, so he said, "They can't go anywhere tonight. To try and go up that mountainside in this storm would be out of the question."

"For them it would be," said Longarm.

"But not for us," Ishir said, understanding Longarm's meaning.

The last thing in the world that Longarm wanted or needed was to climb a mountainside. But he had to admit that the storm would be a perfect cover allowing them to go up to the mansion most likely unseen and unheard. The problem was that he was not sure that he had it left in him to climb even a set of stairs given the awful way he felt.

"Let's tie this one up and go have something to eat and drink at the Green Parrot Saloon," Longarm suggested. "I'm feeling a little weak right now and cold to the bone. Whiskey and some hot food will perk me up."

Ishir nodded and while Longarm watched, the Mongol found some rope and hog-tied the ambusher up so thoroughly that there was no way possible that he could break his bonds and escape.

"You ain't going to just leave me here alone, are you?" the man whined as Ishir was about to stuff his mouth with an oily rag. "There are rats in this place and they'll bite me to pieces."

"It will serve you right," Longarm told the ambusher, thinking that there probably were bold and hungry rats in this big abandoned room. Rats that were surprisingly smart when it came to determining that a living thing was helpless and edible.

160

"You'd better hope that we'll be back," Longarm said with some satisfaction. "Or that the rats find your dead friend in the alley and leave you alone while they feast on Burt."

As he was leaving, Longarm could hear the man thrashing around on the floor, and could even hear his muffled cries over the storm. If the man was attacked by rats, he would probably lose his mind before he lost his life.

But given the pain in Longarm's shoulder and the blood trickling down his left arm, he really did not give a good Gawdamn.

Chapter 24

Longarm and Ishir each devoured three plates of beans and pork, along with an entire loaf of sourdough bread, while sitting beside a red-hot potbellied stove in the Green Parrot Saloon. Longarm had downed a few shots of gut-warming whiskey when he first entered the saloon, then switched to coffee. The Mongol wasn't a drinker and he got John, the saloon owner, to make him a pot of tea.

"What are you men going to do now?" John asked about three o'clock that morning when the storm showed no sign of letting up. "You killed two men tonight. Are you planning to go up that steep, winding road to the mansion and kill the rest of 'em?"

Longarm flexed his throbbing shoulder and stared at the fire crackling through the open door of the stove. "John, I don't know that we want to kill them," he answered. "I'm a United States marshal and I'll give them a chance to surrender."

"Those are tough men up there," John warned.

"The two that tried to drill us from the rooftop also probably thought they were tough," Longarm said. "Now one is lying out there dead and facedown in the mud, and the other is wishing he was dead."

"You mean he *isn't*?" John asked.

Longarm told the saloon owner where the man was hog-tied and gagged. "If we don't make it, then you need to turn that man loose or let him die; it'll be your choice."

Ishir glanced over at the swinging pendulum of the wall clock and said to Longarm, "We've got about three more hours of dark. What do you want to do?"

"Are you game?"

Ishir didn't understand the word, so he shrugged. "What do you mean?"

"I mean," Longarm said, "are you willing to slog up that mountain road before dawn?"

"I am . . . or we could just wait until they come down."

The idea of just waiting out Abby and her gunmen was immensely appealing, but Longarm reluctantly shook his head. "That might not happen for days and I can't wait that long to get back to Denver. Killman may be on another murder hunt and I need to stop him as soon as possible."

The saloon owner looked very skeptical. "Marshal, I'm not trying to tell you your business, but you're both wounded and that storm is still fierce. I've been up that narrow road to the mansion and it's tough even in fair weather. You'll hit both washouts and switchbacks and there's always the risk of mud and rock slides. You'd be crazy to go up blind in this foul weather."

But Longarm wasn't listening. Instead, his thoughts were focused on what they would have to face on the mountainside. "Ishir," he asked, "have you ever shot a gun or rifle?"

The Mongol shook his head and tapped the hilt of his curved knife.

"Well," Longarm said, "I'm sure that you're an expert

with that blade, but it would be a comfort to me if you were armed."

"I've got a double-barreled shotgun he could borrow," John offered. "You just point the thing and pull the triggers. If you're anywhere near your target, it will get blown to bloody smithereens."

"Sounds good," Longarm said. "I've got a sidearm, but I could use a Winchester."

"I'll get you the one that the man dropped on the roof before I grabbed him by the ankles," Ishir said.

"Good enough."

Longarm bought a pint of whiskey, and John was good enough to let him borrow an oilskin slicker. "It won't keep you altogether dry," the saloon owner said, "but it'll be better than nothing in this storm."

"John, why are you offering your help?" Longarm asked. "Those people up at the mansion have probably given you more business than you've had in years."

"That's true," John replied. "But you see, old Zack was my best friend. If those people up at the mansion drill you and that big Chinaman, then Zack died for nothing. I can't stand to have that happen."

"So you're helping us because of Zack?"

"Yeah, and also because there's something wrong with that setup. I've never met the Widow Stanton, but I've seen her passing through town on her way up the mountainside a time or two."

"Her real name is Abby McCall," Longarm explained. "She was never married to Milburn Stanton . . . she was only his assistant. We're pretty sure that either she or this fella named Killman, or maybe even a corrupt Denver police officer, poisoned Mr. Stanton for his land holdings and money."

"Is that a fact?"

"It is," Longarm assured the man. "Although I'm short on proof, there isn't much doubt in my mind."

"Mr. Stanton had a fortune."

"That's right," Longarm said.

"Then why didn't the woman and this Killman fella just take the money and leave the state? Go to Europe or someplace instead of coming here to Black Canyon?"

Longarm had given that very question considerable thought. "I can't say for sure," he replied. "But my guess is that Abby needs to stick close in order to sign some papers and complete the legal part of receiving the full inheritance. And if it is true that Killman went to Denver, it most likely means that there is at least one more target that needs eliminating. That's why we've got to get up that mountainside and arrest Abby McCall, so we can stop her assassin from killing anyone else."

"There are two good riding mules owned by an old miner just outside of town," John said. "They're surefooted and I'm sure the owner would rent them to you cheap. Especially when he finds out what happened to Zack."

"I dunno," Longarm said, not relishing the idea of riding a mule up a soggy mountainside in the dark.

"I'd do it if I were you," John advised. "That mountain road is even longer and steeper than it looks from down here in town. Those mules will keep their footing better'n a man and they can see like cats in the dark. No offense, Marshal, but you look mighty tired and frayed around the edges."

Longarm had to admit that the idea had some merit after hearing this man talk. "I don't know that we could even find that miner in this damned storm."

"You probably couldn't," John said. "So I'll take you to his place."

Longarm drained his last cup of coffee and slowly dipped his chin in agreement. "I suppose we could try mules. If they don't work out, we'd just turn them loose and continue up the road on foot."

"Now you're talking good sense," John said, untying his bar apron and reaching down to get the shotgun.

It was after four in the morning when they roused the old miner and convinced him that his mules wouldn't be shot to death. Longarm paid the man five dollars and said, "We'll turn them loose before we get to the mansion. That's a promise."

It was clear that the old miner really needed the five dollars, but it was also obvious that he was very attached to his pair of mules. "My big mule is stronger than two oxen, but he'll struggle to carry that huge Chinaman."

"He's *not* Chinese," Longarm said, knowing that it didn't matter. To this man and to most others, Ishir looked Oriental and so he was a Chinaman, not a Mongol from the Gobi Desert.

The miner agreed when he learned about the death of his friend Zack. "Just do what needs doin' up there," he told Longarm when the mules were both saddled. "I knew that bunch up there was a den of rattlesnakes even if the woman is pretty enough to take a man's breath away."

"You ever ride a mule?" Longarm asked the giant Mongol, who was studying the big mule with a dubious expression.

"No."

"Not much different than a horse, really."

"I've never ridden a horse either," Ishir admitted. "Is it strong enough to carry me up that mountainside? I'd rather walk."

167

"Suit yourself, but those slick-soled sandals aren't going to be of any use in the mud. You won't be able to get traction."

"Then I'll climb barefooted."

"Chinaman, that's a rocky road," the miner said. "Might lame you. My mules are shod with iron all around."

Longarm added, "Ishir, I know you're skeptical about riding a mule, but I promise you they're going to help and they have better vision in the dark."

"All right," Ishir agreed. "But if this beast starts to slip or stumble, I'm getting off and walking."

"Fair enough," Longarm said.

So they mounted the mules under a tin-roofed shed and rode out into the storm. Ishir got his sandals wedged into the stirrups, which were far too short. So short that his legs were bent and he reminded Longarm of a huge, resting grasshopper.

"Here, Chinaman," the miner shouted as they started for the mountain road, "wrap yourself in this old piece of canvas. Hell, you ain't even got a hat to sluice off the wet."

"I'm *already* wet," Ishir said, throwing the canvas aside as his mule stepped out in the heavy downpour.

"Just thought you might want to keep that shotgun dry, even if you're too dumb to use it on yourself," the miner said, collecting his discarded piece of canvas from the mud.

Longarm didn't say anything as they rode off. The lightning and thunder had slacked off a bit, but there was enough of it so that he could see the mansion in the flashes.

He hoped they could climb that mountain and not get knocked over the edge by a mud slide or rock slide. And he hoped that they could do it before daybreak. Because if

168

they were caught on that exposed road by the four hired gunmen that Abby still had surrounding her, there would be absolutely no place to hide and no place to run.

They'd be as easy to shoot as a pair of ducks in a shooting gallery.

Chapter 25

Longarm had some trouble getting his mule to start up the mountain road. The animal balked and brayed in protest, but it forged ahead when Longarm slashed it across the rump with his reins. Then, picking its way as carefully as a cat through a briar patch, the mule ducked its head close to the ground and began the long climb.

Once or twice Longarm glanced back at Ishir and the big mule, but the visibility was so poor and his own situation so precarious that he didn't have time to worry about the Mongol. It had begun to rain harder and the footing was slick and as treacherous as anything Longarm had ever navigated. Muddy water poured across the road creating deep sluices. The mule balked and protested every time it had to jump over one of these small gullies filled with water. To make matters worse, in some places the road had been almost completely wiped out and was now covered with thick, moving mud.

But they kept going, and little by little they scaled the mountainside. Longarm felt the mule stumble once and fall to its knees, but the animal jumped up and kept scrambling. Once, a huge boulder crashed somewhere just behind them

171

and Longarm knew if he or Ishir had been in its wild, careening path, they would have been knocked off the mountainside road to a certain death.

At last, the mule came to a halt and absolutely refused to go another step. Longarm slapped it several times with his reins, but the animal would not go a step farther.

"All right," Longarm groused, dismounting on the road, "I guess I'll have to finish this climb on foot."

He dismounted and stood beside the trembling animal feeling guilty for having treated it so hard. "We'd never have gotten so far without you," Longarm told the shaky beast as he pulled out the Winchester from its soggy saddle boot. "And now I'm going to tie your reins over the saddle horn and let you pick your way back down what is left of this road. I hope you make it to the bottom and back to your tin shed."

Ishir appeared in a flash of lightning, and Longarm saw that the Mongol was covered with mud. "My mule wouldn't go any farther, so I dismounted and let it go back maybe a hundred feet from where we're standing."

"Let's wait for another flash of lightning and see why my mule quit going forward," Longarm suggested.

It was perhaps a full minute before another jagged bolt illuminated the mountainside. "Holy cow!" Longarm whispered as he stood on the edge of a racing stream of water that had completely washed out the road. "I wonder how deep this washout is."

"Too deep to cross," Ishir said. "We're either going back or we need to climb straight up the mountainside. The mansion is just above us."

"I'm not turning back after coming this far," Longarm told the Mongol. "Let's finish this tonight."

Ishir nodded in firm agreement, and they attacked the mountainside with the last of their strength. When they topped the switchback and fell into the mud, Longarm knew that they had finally reached the mining mansion.

"Ishir, how is that shotgun?" he panted.

"Its barrels are probably clogged with mud."

"Wash out the front of the barrels," Longarm told his friend.

"Will it blow up in my face?"

"I don't know," Longarm said. "Depends."

"Depends on what?"

"Here," Longarm said, taking the weapon.

He broke the shotgun open, removed the shells, and wiped the mud out of the barrels as best he could before holding them up to the sky. When another bolt of lightning seared the night, Longarm saw two round flashes. He reloaded fresh shells and handed the shotgun to the Mongol saying, "It'll be fine. Point and shoot. That's all you have to do."

Longarm started forward with both hands gripping the Winchester. He didn't know if there was a bunkhouse on the property or if the men all slept somewhere in the mansion, but he guessed he'd find out soon enough. The storm was passing, he could feel it letting up, and he knew that the first light of dawn was coming on fast.

They made it to a stable and Longarm moved into the barn, groping his way in the blackness. He could smell the horses, and they were frightened by the storm and stomping nervously around in their stalls.

"Easy," he crooned. "Easy."

Longarm had matches, but he knew they would be wet and useless, so when he found a pile of straw, he slumped down and waited for the first light of day.

"Sleep," Ishir advised. "I'll keep watch."

"I was about to suggest you do the same," Longarm said. He managed a weary and crooked smile. "Wouldn't it be a sonofabitch if we both fell asleep and were found and shot to death."

"It wouldn't be good," Ishir said, not appreciating the gallows humor.

So they sat on the straw and listened to the stomping of horses and the rain as it finally began to slacken. And when a cold, weak light was cast down through the broken clouds from the east, Longarm moved to the barn door and surveyed the mansion.

"Let's take 'em while they're still sleeping," he told the Mongol. "Let's do it right now."

Ishir nodded in agreement. Longarm was surprised at how terrible the Mongol looked covered with mud and with his face haggard with weariness.

And I'll bet I look even worse, he thought as he levered a shell into the Winchester and marched like a rusty tin soldier across the mud to the mansion.

Chapter 26

Longarm and Ishir slogged through the mud to the back of the mansion and let themselves into a big kitchen and pantry, which was still shrouded in almost total darkness. They held their breath and listened, hearing loud snoring in a room down the hallway.

"That isn't Abby," Longarm whispered to the Mongol. "So it must be her hired gunmen and they're still asleep. Follow me and be sure and keep your finger off the shotgun's triggers. And don't shoot unless I do first."

Since this was going to be close work, Longarm rested the wet and muddy Winchester against the wall and drew his Colt. His sodden boots squished and squeaked with every careful step, but that couldn't be helped. The light was so poor that he could barely see to make his way down the hallway.

Because of the darkness he blundered into a coat or hat rack . . . he couldn't tell which. He grabbed blindly for the thing, but it crashed onto the floor.

Suddenly, the snoring stopped and he heard a voice cry out in alarm. Longarm blundered forward wishing that it was he who had the shotgun and not the Mongol, who was right on his heels.

With one hand trailing along the wall, he at last felt a doorway, which he was sure opened into a big sleeping room. Longarm stopped and the Mongol collided into his back.

"Give me the shotgun," Longarm hissed, dreading the powerful weapon's recoil and the amount of pain and additional physical damage it would cause his already badly injured shoulder.

The Mongol didn't argue. He hadn't wanted any part of the unfamiliar, heavy, short-barreled weapon from the start.

Longarm was glad he had decided to take the shotgun, because it was an older-model 8-gauge shotgun whose hammers had to be cocked back before you pulled the triggers and fired. He hadn't told Ishir about this, and it would have been a fatal oversight.

Just beyond the door, he could hear mass confusion and several men shouting. A bar of thin light suddenly flared from under the door.

"So much for the element of surprise," Longarm whispered.

"So what now?"

"We go in and make the arrest."

Longarm stepped aside from the doorway and shouted, "I'm a federal marshal and you men are under arrest. Put your hands in the air and come on out and you won't be hurt."

"Go to hell!" a voice cried.

Longarm heard glass breaking and knew that some of the gunmen were going to escape through a window. If that happened and they scattered on the grounds, it would be far more dangerous trying to catch or kill them, so he found the door handle.

"Ishir, this is going bad, so I'm going in and I'll hit the floor firing."

"What am I supposed to do?"

Longarm said, "If they kill me, then kill them all any way you can as fast as you can."

He didn't wait for the Mongol to answer. Longarm threw open the door and dove inside, hitting the floor with the big 8-gauge shotgun pointing into the room.

One of Abby's hired gunmen was already partway out of the window, and another stood right behind him to be next. Longarm swung the shotgun in their direction and pulled one of the triggers. The slamming kick of the big shotgun against his wounded shoulder was so painful he nearly passed out. Smoke and flame shot across the room and the two men by the window were torn nearly in half. The man half in and half out of the window was hurled into the yard.

For a moment, Longarm couldn't see anything as he struggled to remain conscious. But when one of the gunmen cursed and fired into the doorway, Longarm managed to grit and point. He pulled the second trigger, and the gunfighter was hurled off his feet and into a back wall with the entire upper part of his body resembling a featureless mass of flesh and blood.

The last killer standing lowered his pistol through the blood and the smoke to drill Longarm, but Ishir was through the open doorway and on him in less than a heartbeat. Longarm had to look away because there was nothing good about watching a man's head being severed from his body to then bounce and roll across the floor. The head stopped not three feet from Longarm's face, and that was when he passed out cold.

When Longarm awoke, it was late afternoon and the sun was shining through an upper-floor bedroom window. Longarm's shoulder was heavily bandaged, and he was lying in a bed with Ishir sprawled in a soft chair watching him.

Longarm's head was spinning and he felt as if he were on fire.

"You've got a high fever," Ishir said, stating the obvious. "And you lost a lot of blood. Why didn't you tell me that shotgun had such a kick? I should have used it, not you."

"After seeing what you did with your knife on the last fella's neck, I have to agree. Did you find Abby?"

"Yes. She tried to kill me, but failed."

"Where is she now?"

"Locked up in her bedroom." When he saw Longarm's look of alarm, the Mongol quickly added, "I tied her hand and foot to the bedposts just in case she had any ideas of trying to jump from the second story."

"She's brave enough and now desperate enough to attempt that," Longarm said. "Now I need to get a full confession."

"Can't it wait?" Ishir asked. "You were delirious only a few hours ago."

"It could wait, but I won't let it," Longarm told the giant. "Please bring her to me."

Five minutes later, Ishir hauled Abby McCall into the bedroom. Longarm had expected her to be fighting mad, but she wasn't. Instead, she seemed calm and resigned to whatever fate now awaited her in a Denver courtroom.

"I'm glad that you're not dead," Abby said, taking a seat beside Longarm, who was still lying flat on his back. "I never wanted you hurt. You have to believe at least that much about me."

"I don't," Longarm told her. "Or if you are telling the

178

truth, it is only because it didn't further your plan to get rich."

She shrugged. "I knew you wouldn't understand. You see, Custis, I devoted years to helping Mr. Stanton. In the last few months of his life, it was . . . not pleasant. In fact, it was terrible. Everyone thought of him as so sweet, but when Milburn became infirm, he turned into a demanding tyrant. I had to do things to him that I'd never done for any man. Disgusting things."

"Spare me the details," Longarm told her. "All that matters is that you decided that you had the right to poison him."

"It's clear that you don't understand and never will, so I'm not saying anything more," she told Longarm. "Unless it's to my lawyer."

"Fair enough. You'll meet him behind bars as soon as we get you to Denver."

"You've got *nothing* on me."

"Abby, that's where you're completely wrong," Longarm told her. "We can tie the poison to you because it was in your safe. A jury will have no trouble sentencing you to the gallows given that and the other evidence we've collected."

Abby paled only slightly. She looked over at Ishir and then back at Longarm. She reached out and her soft fingers stroked Longarm's drawn and mud-streaked face. One hand started to slip under his shirt, but Longarm grabbed it hard and pushed it away. "That won't work this time, Abby."

"Have you already forgotten that we were very good together? I doubt you've had anything better than me in your bed. That hasn't changed."

"You were pretty special," he admitted. "But that's in the past and before I knew you were a *murderess*."

The word seemed to hit her hard, but Abby recovered quickly. "Custis, lest you forget, I'm now a rich woman. I could make you very rich, too. And there'd even be money for your Chinese friend. He could go back to wherever he was born and buy a Gawdamn castle and have a hundred young slaves."

"He's Mongolian and he wants to go back to raising sheep."

"I don't care what he is!" she snapped, composure breaking. "I'm offering you a fortune right here and now. Use your head, Custis. We're nothing without money. Join me and we'll travel the world like royalty and have money to burn."

"No, thanks. I'd always wonder if there was something in my last drink that you added."

Abby swallowed hard and her face twisted with bitterness. "So you're going to testify against me and then laugh when I hang. Is that it?"

"I'll testify and you'll hang, all right. But I won't laugh. I might even shed a tear."

"Stuff it!" she cried, sobs beginning to rack her body.

Longarm didn't know what to say. He had never been able to stand watching a woman cry, even an evil one like Abby McCall.

"Please get her . . . get her a glass of water," he told the Mongol. "And a towel or something to dry her face."

Ishir already had a pitcher resting on the bedside table. He poured a glassful of water and gave it to Abby. She stared at it a moment, then stood up and walked over to the window to stare out at the valley and Black Canyon far below. There was a rainbow over in the east and it made her smile ever so slightly "So it's over," she said more to herself than to Longarm.

Her back was to them, and Longarm realized too late

that she was taking something out of her bodice and pouring it into the glass of water.

"Ishir, stop her!" he shouted, trying to move.

The Mongol had been looking away, perhaps because he also could not bear a woman's tears. But none of that mattered because they were both too late. Abby quickly swirled the glass, mixing water with poison, and then she threw it down her throat as if it was the world's most expensive French champagne.

Longarm groaned as Abby turned and faced them to say, "He's out in the mine, you know."

"Who, Abby? Who are you talking about?"

"Why, Dirk Killman, of course." She shivered and swallowed several times, visibly paling. "He was going to kill me and take everything he could get his hands on, so I killed him first. Bullet in the . . . the stomach. He died cursing me, and I watched and laughed."

Abby staggered and grabbed the windowsill. "I almost did them *all* in. If you hadn't come, I would have poisoned the last of the bastards downstairs." She gasped with pain and her eyes rolled. "But you saved me . . . the trouble. Thank you for that at least."

Ishir started to move toward the woman, but he stopped. Longarm pushed himself into a sitting position. "Abby!"

Her eyes burned intensely for an instant and her last words were, "Marshal Custis Long, my real name is *Frances*. Miss Frances Applewhite of New York City. Frances, my mother told me, means free. And now . . . now I *am* free."

She released her grip on the windowsill, stood up as straight as a soldier, then pitched forward dead before she even struck the hardwood floor.

Two days later, Longarm and Ishir had the bodies hauled down the nearly impassable road to Black Canyon, where they were buried without ceremony in the empty mining town's forgotten little cemetery.

Ishir had a faraway look in his eyes as he gazed out past the unmarked graves, and Longarm saw that he was looking west . . . maybe all the way to Asia.

"Ishir?"

The giant turned around, and Longarm said, "Denver is to the east, but you want only to go west. To Mongolia. Isn't that true?"

Ishir nodded, and Longarm opened a saddlebag stuffed with precious jewelry and cash. He removed a bundle of cash and absently reached in and grabbed a handful of jewelry. "Mr. Stanton is dead and who knows where this will all wind up? So take this cash and these jewels and make your long way back home."

Ishir stared at the great wealth that was being offered for at least a full minute, emotions flowing across his broad face like clouds moving across the sun, and then . . . then *he took it.*

Longarm watched Ishir as the huge Mongol started walking home . . . to the West. It was the first really good thing Longarm had seen in quite a while, and it made him feel good and it made him very happy.

Watch for

LONGARM AND THE MISSING MARSHAL

the 335th novel in the exciting LONGARM
series from Jove

Coming in October!

**Explore the exciting Old West with one
of the men who made it wild!**

LONGARM

GIANT-SIZED ADVENTURE FROM AVENGING ANGEL LONGARM.

COMING↓IN↓NOVEMBER 2006...

LONGARM AND THE OUTLAW EMPRESS
0-515-14235-2

WHEN DEPUTY U.S. MARSHAL CUSTIS LONG STOPS
A STAGECOACH ROBBERY, HE TRACKS THE BAN-
DITS TO A TOWN CALLED ZAMORA. A HAVEN FOR
THE LAWLESS, IT'S RULED BY ONE OF THE MOST
⊠POWERFUL, BRILLIANT, AND BEAUTIFUL WOMEN
IN THE WEST...A WOMAN WHOM LONGARM WILL
HAVE TO FACE, UP CLOSE AND PERSONAL.

J. R. ROBERTS

THE GUNSMITH

Available wherever books are sold or at
penguin.com